# LITTLE SIP OF SIN

## CREATURE CAFE SERIES (2)

### CLIO EVANS

*TRIGGER WARNINGS*

## THE BARISTA

It wasn't very often that I was stumped. I folded my tattooed arms across my burly chest and listened to my client.

"I don't even care if I share them with another. I just... I'm ready to find my mate. I'm jealous of my friend. Hell, I even made fun of him when he first brought his mate home. But... I've lived the life of a bachelor long enough. I want someone who can...who can take everything I have to offer."

I pushed my glasses up my nose and did my best not to look down at his crotch. It was a fight, one that I almost lost.

I knew exactly what this dragon shifter meant by those words.

In our world of monsters and humans, creatures like dragons *could* mate with mortals. Even though they were often blessed, or cursed, with size. Not just cock size, but their entire body. They could be in a more human form, and then shift half, and then fully.

Already, this guy was bigger than my cooler door. He had half shifted once we were alone, as holding a full human form was extremely difficult for long periods of time.

"I see. Man? Woman?" I asked.

"Either. Both. I don't care, Barista."

I nodded and raised a brow. "You really don't mind sharing?"

My client shrugged and even smiled a little. A little flame escaped his mouth as he licked his lips.

Ah.

Now, I understood.

It wasn't that he didn't mind sharing. He wanted to share.

Most creatures were extremely possessive. I guessed that my client would be— but that they also wanted the experience of being with more than one soul.

Needy bastard. It was a challenge, but I liked challenges.

"You realize that you're asking for two mates— not just one?" I questioned, leaning against the wall. Surrounding the two of us were bags of beans from a farm in Ethiopia run by a Sphinx and his wife (who was a panther shifter).

"I know. But I know that you can work wonders. You were able to find someone to love my roommate, and hell — that must have been hard."

I snorted. It hadn't been *that* hard. Peter and Dante were meant for each other.

"Give me some time," I said, raising a brow at him. "Give me a month. It's longer than what it usually takes me, but it's necessary. I have to get all the right pieces in the right places. I'll leave you a voicemail."

"Okay," he said, giving me a patient smile.

The patience was...well, I wondered how long it would be before I saw him in my cafe asking about my search.

I had no doubts. My wheels were already turning, searching for the right matches.

Three souls.

I had another client that had said something similar just earlier this week.

It was funny how much fate had to say in my work. I was just the pen, and destiny was the ink. Even the darkest of creatures had a yearning in them— a yearning to be cared for. To be loved.

Even Hades had a soulmate.

"Alright. Get out of here," I said, jerking my head towards the door. I was tired of being locked in my cooler with a horny dragon. "I'll be in touch."

"Thanks," he said. He shoved open the cooler and was out in a blink.

I followed him out and watched him barrel out of the cafe.

It was a quiet, snowy night. The crisp air made its way into the warm space every time the door opened but was quickly doused by the heat. The cafe was quiet this evening, with people stopping by here and there to pick up something hot. More humans than usual as well.

It made sense. A lot of creatures hibernated during this time of the year or moved somewhere warmer. Bear shifters, werewolves, hell hounds...All of them hated the snow.

Well, except for my werewolf friend Al.

But Al was weird.

"BARISTA!"

I jumped as one of my waitresses damn near tackled me. She grabbed my arms and shook me, despite the fact she was at least two feet shorter than me.

"Dante and Peter! They're here! You have to say hi!"

"Breathe," I said, shaking her off. "Good god, you'd think the king of the universe was here. I'll go say hi."

"They have a surprise!" she squealed.

For a moment, I wondered if my glass windows would break. I gave her a look that forced her to regain composure and then went out into the cafe to see my old client and his love.

Seeing them together was picturesque. I paused for a moment, smiling.

Finding two souls for my new client would be hard, but it would be worth it.

Plus, it'd be two birds and one stone.

I smirked to myself and then went to greet my two friends.

**KAT**

I stood on the corner of Main Street and Fang Lane, which was a fitting road to hold Creature Cafe. I could see the glass of the windows gleaming in the morning light, the neon sign burning like a fuchsia flame.

It looked so damn innocent. To the human world— it was just a quaint hipster cafe.

To the world of monsters, it was the place everyone went to gossip and to, surprisingly, find love.

I had told myself for months that I would never ever *EVER* accept an invitation from the Barista, and yet here I was. Dressed to the nines in black leather leggings, boots with heels, and a tunic that hugged me in all the right places. Part of being a snow baby was that you figured out how to use layers to accentuate what god gave you, and I had mastered that art pretty well.

I had sworn off love for years now, but somehow...somehow, the bastard had found the right moment to leave a voicemail on my phone.

*Hey Kat, I wanted to let you know that I have found you the perfect dates. Come to my cafe on February 1st at 10am. Don't be late and don't argue. You owe me one, and this is good for you.*

It was like he knew my heart had shriveled up to the size of a grinchy walnut.

The thing was— he was right. I did owe him one, and it *would* be good for me. I hadn't gone on a date in god knew how long. Long enough that the boots I wore had a fine layer of dust on them when I had dug them out of my closet.

Long enough that the Brazilian I had gotten had actually brought tears to my eyes.

It had been hard after Cal had died.

My heart ached for a moment. I was a picture, wasn't I? A little woman mourning her lost man on the corner of a street.

I had promised myself I wouldn't think about him, but I couldn't help it.

He would want me to move forward with this. He would want me to move on.

I deserved to be happy, and I was tired of cockblocking myself.

How long had it been since I'd had a good tumble?

I snorted and finally crossed the street. I'd be a couple of minutes late, but...the Barista didn't control me.

I flipped my hair as I pulled open the cafe door and stepped inside.

"You're late."

God damn it.

I almost ran straight into the tattooed ginger mountain known as the Barista. He glowered down at me.

"They're over there at the table. I should spit in your coffee for being late, but I'm feeling merciful today."

"Oh god, you're so dramatic," I sighed, fighting the urge to roll my eyes.

I squeezed past him and ignored the string of curses under his breath. As soon as I made my way around him, I stopped.

My heart squeezed, my head feeling light.

Why was my heart beating so fast? It felt like I was on a racetrack in the fastest car, and someone had yanked the brakes out.

Lounging in two lush chairs at a small table were two of the most gorgeous men I had ever seen in my life.

One of them had dark golden skin with glints of indigo scales here and there, long black hair, strong brows, and eyes that burned like drops of sunshine. He looked like an Egyptian god.

The other had dirty blonde hair that was short, a chiseled face, eyes the color of emeralds, and skin that was covered in a rainbow of scales. He was more shifted than the other, and even from where I stood, I could see the hint of his fangs in the morning light.

Dragon shifters.

My stomach gave an uneasy pull, my pussy throbbing.

*Easy girl,* I hissed at myself.

The one with golden eyes looked up at me and smiled.

Warmth filled me, followed by heat.

Fuck.

I heard a snicker from behind the counter and knew that the Barista was laughing at me.

I finally shook myself and walked towards them. "Sorry I'm late," I said, offering them both a smile.

"No worries," the green-eyed one said, standing. "My name is Verdell, although you can call me Dell."

Good god, that accent. What was it? British? Every word had a lilt to it. My pussy was beginning to flutter.

He offered me his hand, and I took it. Electricity ran up my arm and then straight back down to my crotch.

God damn it, I was already getting wet.

This was crazy! Insane!

I was confused as hell as to why there were two of them here, but...I wasn't going to complain. I had never had anything against loving more than one person, and if the Barista really thought this might work out, then maybe...

"My name is Dracon," the other said, grinning. "You look...divine."

"Thank you," I said, pulling my hand from Dell. "My name is Kat."

"Kat..." Dell hummed as if he were trying out my name. The tip of his tongue paused on one of his fangs, and then he grinned.

Oh, he was a charmer.

"Let me take your coat," Dracon said, moving behind me.

I let him take off my coat, which might have been a mistake. As soon as he touched me, I felt that same pull that I felt from Dell.

Holy fuck, I wanted to do *really* bad things to both of them. The type of things that a priest would drown me in holy water for.

Dracon's hands lingered for a moment, and then he let out a soft breath. It was edged with a noise, almost a growl.

I let out a nervous laugh, and the three of us sat down.

The two of them already had coffee in front of them, and I was about to turn to find a waitress, but she was already bringing over my regular.

Dracon raised his dark brows as she handed it to me. "I'm guessing you come here often?" he asked.

"Yes," I admitted, smiling.

I was here at least three times a week, actually.

"I, uh...I love coffee. It's kind of an addiction." That was an understatement. "And creatures," I said, blushing. "I like creatures."

Dell leaned back in his chair, studying me. He wasn't bashful about it either. He took me in hungrily, his gaze sweeping my face, my breasts, and then my legs.

I studied him back, unashamed. For a moment, I wondered how the chair was holding his massive form. His shoulders were wider than a linebacker's.

"I didn't expect...I didn't expect there to be two people," I said, pulling my gaze from Dell to Dracon.

"Well," Dracon said, quirking his brow again. "I had told the Barista I wasn't against sharing...."

"I also said the same. The man is a bit evil, I think," Dell chuckled, leaning forward. His knee was less than a centimeter from mine, and somehow that created more sexual tension than I had ever felt before. "Two dragon shifters with a human," he said, his eyes glinting.

"I could handle you," I said, dismissive of what he meant. "Both of you," I said, tipping my chin up.

"I'm sure you could, kitten," he said, his voice dangerously low.

Kitten. Oh, fuck.

"Hmmm," Dracon hummed. "I think... I'm sure you could handle us. How did you learn about creatures?"

Us. They had already bonded, despite the fact that they

hadn't known each other either. I ran the tip of my tongue over my bottom lip and felt Dracon's eyes follow it.

"Well. Like most humans who discover creatures, I learned about them the hard way. My friend Cal was eaten by an out-of-control werewolf. I'm pretty certain that the moon was high, and we had stumbled upon him feeding. I don't remember much," I said. My words had dissolved into a whisper, and I felt my eyes tear up. "Uh...But, it was like — once I realized werewolves were real, I couldn't stop seeing others. I got in quite a bit of trouble, but the Barista helped me out. Helped me learn. Hell, I even worked here for a few months a long time ago to get my feet back under me."

Calling Cal my friend was a soft lie, but I didn't want the pity. Losing a friend and losing someone you were supposed to marry were similar, but people's reactions were violently different.

"I wish I would have been here then," Dracon whispered. His gaze flickered for a moment as if he was shouldering the blame. "I'm sorry your friend died."

"I am too, Kat. It's tragic that most humans learn about us in ways like that," Dell said, studying me. "But, regardless, I am glad that you're here. And that you're open to... being with creatures like us."

I nodded and took a sip of my coffee. *God damn it.*

I made a face and turned to glare over my shoulder.

"What happened?" Dracon asked, sounding alarmed.

The Barista winked at me and then disappeared into the back.

"He put almond milk in my latte because he knows I don't like it. It's because I was late," I said, glaring. The glare then melted into a devious giggle. "It's fine. I'll get him back later."

"So, you actually *know* him?" Dell asked, cocking his head.

Was there a hint of jealousy there?

"No," I sighed, "Well. Perhaps. Enough to know that I'm going to get back at him later. But, anyways...tell me about you. Being a dragon shifter must be...." I trailed off, engulfed by his eyes. I felt like he was staring straight into my soul. Straight into my mind.

A hand touched my thigh, and I looked over at Dracon. Heat speared me, my words lost to the void of lust.

"You feel it too?" he whispered.

Feel it? Yeah, I felt it. I felt like my heart was about to explode, my mind about to implode, and my pussy about to cum harder than it ever had.

I made a sound and nodded, swallowing hard.

"At least I'm not crazy then," he laughed, drawing his hand back.

Dell snorted, smirking. "I think you'll find you like us, Kat," he said. "Dracon and I have already talked about how this will work."

"Oh yeah?" I asked.

"Yes. You see. Dracon has roommates. I don't. And I have a very large home with many bedrooms. How do you feel about getting away for the weekend? We could all three get to know each other and explore...things. You could leave at any point if you chose to. And of course— we won't eat you," Dell said.

The twist of his lips told me otherwise.

Well, maybe he wasn't going to eat me.

But, he *was* going to *devour* me.

Before I knew what I was saying, I spoke. "Yes."

"Good then," Dracon said, letting out a soft sigh. "Perfect."

"I'll prepare for guests then," Dell said with a grin.

I nodded and blinked, trying to think clearly.

What the hell had I gotten myself into?

**DELL**

"Are you going to be a good little dragon for me?" Dracon growled as he gripped my cock, slamming me against the wall. I moaned and arched, exposing my neck to him.

His wings stretched behind him, the indigo shining brilliantly. His eyes burned, his touch heated. He leaned in, his fangs latching onto my neck.

"Yes," I gasped, bucking against him.

Pain burned through me for a moment, followed by the pleasure of taking a dragon bond. The two of us had barely made it to the weekend, and he had come over before Kat.

We were both eager to take her and to take each other.

How long had I lived? How long had I searched for another? Finally, the Barista had not only found me one but two souls.

Blood dripped down my neck, and I moaned, licking my lips. My cock was pulsing in his burly grip.

The two of us were so close to coming undone. Dracon's

skin glinted in the light, his scales shining. His golden eyes drew me in, capturing me.

"I'm going to end up shifting," I panted. I was on the edge of control, so damn close to falling apart.

"Shift then. I want to see what *it* looks like," he growled. My crimson blood wet his lips, and I watched the tip of his tongue swipe it away.

"Hello?"

The two of us froze. Kat's voice echoed through my house.

"Hello? Dell? Dracon?"

She was so damn cute and innocent and...

Dracon leaned in and brushed his lips over the mark he had just left, his magic healing the wounds in a blink. He winked at me and left me standing there, my cock hard and body ready to burst at the seams. I watched him disappear down the stairs, his greeting echoing through my house.

I looked down at my throbbing hard-on and blew out a breath. I took a few moments and then reached down, adjusting my waistband. Finally, when I felt like my shaft wasn't completely apparent, I moved down the stairs and into my living room.

Kat was standing at the center, looking around with wide eyes. Her blonde hair fell in shiny waves, her heart-shaped face tipped up. She had painted her lips a bright red, and I fought the urge to run to her and kiss her. She was wearing sexy heels, black pants, and a top that really hugged her curves.

She knew how hot she was. She knew exactly how to accentuate her body. I appreciated how comfortable she seemed to be in her own skin.

In that way, she was like a dragon shifter. Most dragons took great pleasure in their appearance, myself included.

We knew that we were sexual. We knew that we were beautiful.

Dracon must have gone to the kitchen because I heard movement coming from that direction.

Years of solitude made me feel grateful to hear the echoes of others.

Kat turned, her face lighting up. I grinned as I went up to her, raising a brow. "What do you think, kitten?"

Her eyes flashed at the nickname, her lips parting. She gave me a slow smile. "Your house is beautiful. Who knew a dragon shifter would be so modern," she teased.

I looked around and shrugged. I was used to my home. I had designed every piece of it. It was exceptionally modern, but I had always enjoyed simplicity. There was also the open airiness of the house— the openness that allowed me to shift without breaking things.

Did I tell her about the room below the house?

Her eyes wandered around and then came back to me. Everything about her was magnetic, drawing me in. I wanted to take her then and there, but it was too soon.

She was mine. Just as Dracon was mine.

The weekend was going to be perfect.

"Here you go," Dracon said, bringing three glasses of wine from the kitchen.

We both took from one him, and I raised a brow. He had put his wings away, morphing back into his most human-looking form.

He gave me a knowing look, one that made my cock twitch.

"A toast," she said, beaming.

"To us," I said.

"To finding love," Dracon proposed.

Kat's brows drew together. "I don't know about that, but this will be fun, I'm sure."

The two of us gave each other a side look. There was a glint of challenge reflecting in his golden gaze now.

She would be hard to convince, but we could do it. Perhaps because she was a human, she didn't feel the absoluteness that we both felt.

She took a sip of the wine, her cheeks turning a bit pink. I realized that I was staring at her, and watching the flush overcome her golden skin was addicting. I wanted to watch that flush as she rode on top of me...

My cock pulsed again, and I let out a breath. I had to get ahold of myself.

Kat's eyes fell down to my crotch, and I heard her breath hitch. "Hmm...I see," she said. She took a step closer, the warmth of her body clinging to me. "We're here to have fun, right?" she whispered.

Dracon stepped behind her, and she gave us both a wicked little smile.

Dracon let out a little moan. "I think we wanted to ease into it, but if you keep teasing us, then I'm going to make you suck his cock while I eat you out."

Her eyes lit up, and she arched her head back to look at him, exposing her throat entirely to me.

I was frozen in place, watching their exchange.

Dracon's hand lifted, and he cupped her throat, his talons giving the slightest squeeze.

"I want both of you. It's all I've thought about this entire week. I've come home from work wet because of the fantasies that are plaguing me."

I let out a low growl, my chest rumbling. My grip on the wine was becoming too much, the glass threatening to shatter.

Dracon's grip tightened, and she let out a choked breath.

"Tell me," he said darkly. "Do you really know what you're getting yourself into? We're not human, Kat. We're dragons. We mate for life. And we both want you. There's no turning back after today, even though you think this is fun and games."

I stepped closer to her and traced the tip of my own talon from the base of her throat, down her chest, to between her breasts. She let out the smallest whimper.

"You want to be worshipped," I whispered. "And we will worship every part of you. I bet I can even make you cum standing here," I taunted. "But before we start that, we both need to know what your limits are."

"Limits?" she asked.

Dracon slowly let go of her neck, and she looked at me. Now her entire face was red, her eyes burning with heat. I reached forward and twisted my fingers in her golden hair.

"Woman, we're going to devour you," I whispered, giving the strands a tug.

"We can use red for stop, yellow for slow, and green for go," she said quickly. She held the glass of wine to her lips and tipped it back.

I'd never seen someone down wine like a shot, and it amused me.

A drop escaped her lips, and before she could catch it, I leaned forward and licked it up with my tongue. My tongue was forked at the end, allowing me to taste the wine and her flesh.

Her moan, the wine, the taste of her skin— all of it was sweet.

Dracon swept her hair back and leaned down, running his lips down the side of her neck. I enjoyed watching him, the way his dark brows drew together. The way his pupils became diamond shapes as his hunger grew.

"Little kitten," I growled. "Look at her, Dracon. She's already ours."

He growled in agreement.

I plucked the glass from her hand and his and carried them over to a small table. I set them down and turned to look at the two of them.

Most creatures would be jealous, but seeing his massive body pressed against her— seeing the way he kissed her— all of it made me unbelievably hard. I wanted to be buried inside of her while he fucked me. I wanted to know what it would feel like for her to try and fit my dragon cock in her pretty little mouth.

Dracon let out a frustrated sound and took a step back, his gaze flickering to me. "We were supposed to be patient."

"I want this," Kat said, looking at both of us. "You don't need to be gentle with me. If I didn't want this, I wouldn't have shown up. I trust the Barista, and I trust that he paired the three of us up for a reason. And not only that— I really really *really* want to be fucked right now."

All of the tension in the room broke, and I felt my own reservations crumble. I moved quickly and scooped her up. She let out a squeal of surprise as I threw her over my shoulder. Her body was as light as a feather to me.

Dracon led the way. I had already shown him the room.

## Dragon

I was falling apart.

My heart hammered in my chest as Kat wound her arms around my neck, drawing me close for our first real kiss. Dell's hands were undressing her, touching her, making her moan. She fell into me a little, her lips brushing mine.

She tasted delicious. I growled as her tongue slipped into my mouth, touching mine.

I could hear her heart beating fast. I could hear the little noises Dell made as he became hotter and hotter.

Our dragons were begging to be released, and it was a fight to not let them out. I could feel his writhing beneath the surface, aching to be seen.

Everything about this felt right. I had my doubts. Hell, I had to be patient too. The Barista had taken his time finding the right ones— and now that I was with both of them, I knew it was worth it.

My cock was throbbing in my pants. I had almost taken

Dell before she arrived. I wanted both of them completely.

Dell had already taken my bond. The dragon within me craved to mark Kat too, urging me to do so now so she could never escape us.

I worried she would run from us once she saw us in our true forms. What if she didn't really like the monsters we were? Dragons were beautiful but frightening. All of the space Dell had in his home would be filled with us.

I'd be able to hold Kat in my jaws.

A shot of pleasure ran through me, and I groaned, the image of her riding my tongue making my balls squeeze.

The three of us tumbled into the room. The playroom. The pleasure room. Curtains were drawn, blocking out most of the sunlight. Kat drew back for a moment, looking around.

A low growl came from Dell as the last of her clothing fell to the floor. I smiled.

Even in the dark, Dell and I could see every part of her. Every curve, every muscle. She was aroused and wet already, her scent making my mouth water.

"Kat," I whispered gruffly.

"You're beautiful," Dell said. I watched him trace his talons across her skin, from the top of her shoulder, and down her arm.

"She is," I purred, tipping her face up.

Her eyes burned in the darkness. She wasn't afraid of us. She wasn't afraid of monsters, even with what had happened to her friend.

She looked up at me, her cheeks flushed. "I want to see...both of you. I'm naked, but you're both clothed. And you're still in your human forms, which I've heard is uncomfortable."

I let out a hiss, completely undone by her words. I

blinked a few times as my vision shifted, the world igniting in the bright hues of heat signatures.

She and Dell were the hottest things in the room.

"*Kitten*," Dell growled.

Before either one of us could move, she reached for me. Her fingers slid over the top of my waistband, and she undid the button. She slid her hand in, gripping my cock.

"Fuck, you're big," she gasped.

That was it. I looked up at Dell, and I watched him let go some. His body began to shift, his clothes ripping. Kat turned to watch, her eyes widening.

Dell took a step back to give himself space as his muscles became hard rainbow-scaled ropes, his emerald wings bursting from his back. His wingspan was something to be admired, even in his half-shifted form. He still had the face of a man, and the body, except now he had a tail, wings, and his skin was completely scaled. His eyes glowed in the darkness, and he parted his lips, wisps of fire shooting out. He then blew.

Torches around the room ignited, bathing the three of us in warm light. There was something erotic about watching him unleash just a hint of his power.

Kat's eyes widened as she looked around.

The room we were in was massive, with ceilings that were about twenty feet high. The walls were lined with mirrors, and against the wall was a massive bed covered in silk sheets and soft blankets.

Then there were the ropes and the restraints. One of the walls had a crucifix installed, and I'd be tying one of them to it later.

"Holy shit," she whispered. She licked her lips, looking at Dell. Her golden hair tumbled down her breasts, her skin already gathering a delicious sheen of sweat.

I shifted next, drawing both of their attention. I let out a low growl as my body expanded.

It felt good. Invigorating to release. Kat became smaller and smaller as I grew, my wings spreading behind me.

I looked down at her and grinned, revealing my sharp teeth. "Are you scared yet, Kitten?"

"No," she breathed, looking from Dell to me and back again.

"Good," I said. "Dell, you should taste her."

I wanted to watch him devour her right now. I could be patient.

I would have both of them soon enough, and the anticipation was tantalizing.

Dell picked her up, drawing out a breathless squeal from her. She was so small in his arms. A fragile little human. Our mate.

I wanted to rut her so badly. My hands slid down to my pulsing cock, to the knot at the base. I gave it a light squeeze and groaned.

I had so much seed to give. My cock would fill up over and over again.

Dell lifted her up in the air until her legs were seated on his massive shoulders. She let out a cry as his tongue plunged into her, the wet sounds filling the room. I moved closer to them, studying her reactions intensely.

Her back arched, her thighs squeezing around his head.

She was already losing herself in us. I grinned, letting out a low rumble. "Eat her good, Dell," I commanded.

His cock was pulsing, vibrant red, and slick. He didn't have the same ridges that I did, and the head was sloped differently.

I loved it. Every dragon's cock was unique, and his was deliciously perfect.

I licked my lips and knelt in front of him, taking it into one of my palms.

He and Kat both let out a groan together.

"Don't move, Dell. I'm going to pleasure you," I whispered.

Kat let out a curse and then another cry. I looked up at her and grinned, watching her first orgasm take her.

Pre-cum was streaming from the tip of his cock. I leaned forward and flicked my tongue over the head. His hips jerked, his cock bobbing.

It was thick and long. In this form, it was already about 12 inches from knot to tip and then a few inches wide.

I gripped it, enjoying the way his hips reacted. I began to pump him slowly with my hand and then leaned in to taste him again.

He tasted sweet. I let out a soft moan and then took him into my mouth. I unhinged my jaw so I could take all of him down my throat.

He paused in his devouring of our mate, his yell filling the room. "Fuck, Dracon, that feels amazing!"

His hips began to thrust, the head of his cock hitting the back of my throat. I squeezed his knot as he humped me, enjoying the way he fucked my mouth.

I could feel him close to coming, so I pulled off. My lips burned from his hot seed.

I grinned, licking them.

"Turn her upside down," I commanded, standing up.

Kat let out a squeal as Dell let her fall back, his tongue still buried in her pussy. I helped lower her and grinned as her gaze met mine, her lips parting in pleasure.

"Hi, little one," I said, cupping her head.

"This feels so good," she moaned, her eyes fluttering.

Dell was holding her by her thighs. I met his burning

gaze and chuckled.

"How does she taste?"

He drew out for a moment, licking around his mouth. "Come find out, Dracon."

I grinned and stepped forth, kissing him. Her taste was on his lips, on his tongue.

Suddenly, a tongue lapped at the head of my cock.

I drew back, looking down at Kat.

She reached for me, her soft little hands taking my shaft.

"Fuck," I growled. "Woman, you're going to undo me."

"I want to taste you," she rasped.

Dell hummed and gripped one of her ankles, drawing her up into the air between us. She started giggling at his display of strength, her entire body flushed.

I reached out and twisted one of her nipples. She gasped, her eyes lighting up.

"Look at you, kitten," he purred, "So fucking wet and eager to taste us."

"Put her on her knees," I said darkly. I ran the tip of my tongue over my sharp teeth.

Dell slowly sat her down on the floor. She rolled over, drawing in steadying breaths for a moment as she got onto her knees.

"Look how perfect you are," I said, grinning.

I felt a sense of pride. Not only had I found a beautiful male dragon, but I had also found the most perfect little human female.

She crawled between the two of our bodies, sitting back on her heels. She reached up, gripping each of our cocks with one of her hands.

Dell and I moaned at the same time.

She began to stroke us, opening her mouth. "I want to

be covered in both of you."

I let out a breath. I had never lived in a more perfect moment.

She began to stroke us vigorously. I ran my hands down Dell's chest, pausing to tweak one of his nipples. His whole body responded, his wings jerking behind him. I began to rub them, enjoying the way his cries became louder and louder.

He was going to cum first. I wanted his milk to bathe her, to drip down her pretty tear-stained cheeks.

"Make him cum," I growled, looking down at her.

Her eyes glinted with mischief, and she leaned forward, running her tongue over his knot. He shuddered, her magic touch forcing him over the edge. His head tilted back as his cock began to spurt streams, splashing over the two of us.

"Fuck," he groaned.

I grinned to myself and then shoved him to the floor. "Clean up your mess. Help him out, Kat."

His eyes were still half-lidded as his tongue snaked out. The two of them leaned forward, their tongues running over my skin. Kat's hands cupped my balls, and I groaned.

"I want you to be inside of me."

I blinked, looking down at Kat. Dell raised both of his eyebrows. "You think he can fit?"

"I want to try," she said, licking her lips. "Please. But I want to see the two of you fuck first."

My lips parted, my heartbeat picking up. I wanted to be inside of her too. Ached to be sheathed in her heat. Fuck. I ached to be inside of Dell as well.

I looked at him, and he gave me the slightest not, his eyes burning with passion.

"Little kitten," I said wickedly. "And my little dragon. Take her to the bed."

**KAT**

I had never been this turned on in my entire life. I let out a squeal as Dell scooped me up in his massive arms and carried me to the bed across the room. His skin was covered in a rainbow of scales, his eyes glittering in the warm light.

He tossed me onto the mattress, and I laughed as I bounced.

Then I felt the heat.

The heat of Dracon's gaze.

The heat of Dell's.

The two dragon shifters stared at me, taking me in. Every time they smiled or opened their mouths, I could see their sharp teeth glinting. Ready to devour me, to take a bite out of my soul.

Not to mention their forked tongues. The fucking forked tongue that had made me cum several times. It had reached inside of me, had stroked me in places a normal man had never even dreamed of touching.

If there was a god, they had done me a favor by giving them those fancy things.

Dell's cum was still smeared across my body, coating me. I let out a heated breath as Dracon reached for Dell, gripping the back of his neck.

Their chemistry was so hot. I let out a small moan as Dracon positioned Dell in front of him, shoving him over the side of the bed.

I was just out of reach of Dell. I spread my legs slowly, my hand sliding down to my clit. I shivered, pleasure sliding through me.

"Fuck, look at you," Dracon whispered to Dell.

Dell let out a moan, his wings lowering. His muscles rippled as Dracon ran his talons down his back and then down the muscled branches that led to the verdant skin of his wings. His tail swept to the side.

How could he be so damn dominant with me and so submissive to Dracon?

Then again, I was just as ready to submit to the golden-eyed dragon. He was alluring, commanding, strong... Beyond sexy.

Dracon's body seemed to grow even more, his shadow casting across the room. He stepped away for a moment and came back with what I could only assume was a monster made condom, fitting it over himself even as he started to shift. His wings raised behind him, the translucent webbing glowing like sapphire with threads of ice.

I began to stroke myself, pushing my fingers inside of me. I was so damn wet from cumming on Dell's tongue. I let out a small pant, moaning.

Dracon's cock was pulsing and was bright orange. Veins ran over it, and the top was covered in ridges. I licked my lips, longing to try and take that thing.

Dell let out the smallest moan.

"Before you arrived, I almost took him," Dracon growled, looking directly at me.

As soon as our eyes met, heat spread through my body. I was so close to the edge again.

"Isn't that right, little dragon?"

"Yes," Dell groaned.

"I wanted to fuck him against the wall. Hard. I wanted to make him scream."

My breath hitched. His wild side was finally starting to unleash.

Both of them were still holding back but now...

I watched a wicked beast overtake him. His pupils were sharp slits, his tongue slipping out like a snake. He was standing at least 9 feet tall now— a massive dragon shifter. His blue scales gave him the appearance of something otherworldly.

He was the master in this room right now. Dell's master. My master.

"I'm going to breed him fucking raw," he rasped. "And then I'm going to take you, little kitten."

He thrust forward, and I watched Dell's expression become euphoric as he took Dracon's massive cock. He yelped, his talons tearing into the blankets. The fabric ripped, his muscles hardening.

Dracon was going to show him no mercy.

He gripped Dell's hair and yanked his head back, reaching around to slip a talon in his mouth. Dell moaned, opening up. Blood dripped from the corner as the edge dug into his lips.

"You deserve this," Dracon growled. "You deserve to be fucked mercilessly, you slut."

His words turned me on even more. *Fuck.*

Dell moaned in agreement, his eyes rolling back in his head from the intensity.

I started grinding against my hand, but it wasn't enough. I looked to my left, to where a pillow was. I grabbed it and slid closer to Dell.

His eyes watched me, but I knew he was barely seeing me. Every thrust from Dracon brought out a yell from him, his entire body taking the force.

I mounted the pillow and began to hump it, running my hands down my body. I rubbed my breasts, wishing that one of them would sink their teeth into me.

Dracon let out a purring noise. It echoed through the room, a soft clicking deep within his throat.

Drool was leaking down Dell's chin, and I leaned forward, licking it up. Dracon let go of his mouth, allowing me to take it.

I kissed him, enjoying the way his tongue felt. He moaned in my mouth and bit my bottom lip.

Pain ran through me— the delicious kind. The kind that made me hump my pillow even harder.

I drew back from his mouth with a gasp.

Dracon's hand suddenly gripped my hair, and he forced me to look at him.

"If you want something to ride, then get your ass on my tail. Now."

Fuck. He let go of me, and I whimpered, my throat dry. Dell let out a yell, his cries becoming louder as Dracon picked up his rhythm. The sound of their skin slapping together followed me as I got down from the bed quickly and crawled across the floor.

I had a perfect view of the two of them joining together. I stopped for a moment, watching Dracon's balls slap against Dell's ass.

They'd asked if I thought he'd fit.

There was no way in hell but damned if I wouldn't try.

"Get on my fucking tail. *Now.* If I have to ask again, I will punish you!" Dracon snarled.

Every girl has dreams about riding a dragon, and damned if that dream wasn't about to come true.

His tail was huge. It was long and thick and covered with soft spikes. I reached out and took one in my palm, gripping it.

I gasped. They were pulsing. And not only were they vibrating, but the temperature was also shifting every few seconds from brutally hot to brutally cold.

It was almost like...

"Holy shit," I whispered.

The way the spikes were spread, I'd be able to take one in each hole...

I moaned and crawled on top of it. One of the spikes brushed against my opening, and I gasped. It was icy, sending a bolt of pleasure straight through my body.

I shifted forward and shuddered as it entered me. It was so fucking cold, but then...then it slowly started to become hot. The vibrations became harder, shifting from a tribal beat to a fucking jackhammer.

"Dracon!" I cried.

Another spike pressed against my ass, and I moaned, teasing the entrance. I slowly took it, letting out a faint scream.

Dracon laughed, "Dell, you should see her. She's fucking my tail."

Dell moaned, still taking Dracon like a champ.

The spikes began to turn cold as I started to ride them, moving my hips. I leaned forward and hugged it, giving me the right angle to bounce up and down.

Pleasure began to build, the vibrations racing through my body. There was another small spike pressing against my clit, pulsing over and over again.

"*Dracon*," I moaned, "This feels so good."

"Fuck," he gasped. He was finally starting to get close to the edge.

I began to ride him harder as he started to thrust into Dell harder until finally, I watched him cum. He let out a roar and buried himself in deep, drawing out a cry from Dell. His muscles twitched as he sank against Dell, their breaths filling the room.

He laid his head on Dell's back for a moment, angling his face so he could look at me. His eyes glowed like golden stars, the scales around his face a beautiful shade of teal.

He let out a soft moan and slowly pulled out of Dell. He pulled the condom off and cum spilled out, the milky drops hitting the floor.

For a brief moment, I prayed that my IUD would be able to withstand the powers of *that*. I wasn't sure if dragon shifters and humans could make babies, but I wasn't ready to find out quite yet.

The spikes began to heat up again, and I couldn't help it — I moaned, tipping my head back. Arms suddenly swept me up, and I was thrown back onto the bed.

Dracon had me pinned under him, the tip of his cock pressing against me.

"You just came!" I exclaimed, shocked.

I heard Dell snicker. Dracon leaned in and kissed me with a dark chuckle. His teeth nicked me, the taste of copper filling my mouth.

He slid down, trailing kisses from my neck now to my breasts. My breath caught, and I reached up, gripping his shoulders.

"I can't treat Dell and ignore you," he murmured, smirking.

His forked tongue flicked across my nipple, and I gasped, writhing beneath him. He began to play with both of them as he held me in place, cleaning up the remnants of Dell's cum.

My pussy throbbed, desperate for attention. He leaned back and splayed my legs, his eyes falling to my clit.

"Look how wet you are," he murmured.

His tail slid around me, curling around my chest. He bound my arms close to my side.

I tried to move, but the tail was like a thick straight jacket, not allowing me to break free. He grinned down at me, and I felt a flicker of...

Not fear. Something else. Adrenaline. A rush. I was completely *his* in every way. He was in control of my body, and I was at his complete mercy.

He was a monster, a creature. He would take me however he pleased.

Dracon's talons shifted back, revealing more human-like fingers. His hand slid down to my pussy, and he pushed two in slowly, spreading me. My muscles tensed, my head tipping back. The rest of me was held completely still.

It didn't matter how hard I jerked against him, he held me in place.

"So wet," he rasped.

He drew his fingers out, and I watched him lick them clean.

"Mmm, you taste so good, little one," he murmured. "I'm going to use some magic on you to keep you from...."

"Dying?" I rasped, trying to buck my hips against him.

He laughed, enjoying the power he had over me.

I heard Dell laugh too and looked at him. He was...

My eyes widened. He had shifted completely. I realized that behind Dracon was the full glory of Dell taking up the rest of the room. His enormous head moved behind Dracon, his eyes peering down at me. They were an even brighter green than his wings. Another deep chuckle filled the room.

The way they looked at me was enough to almost make me cum. I panted, whining. "You're huge," I gasped.

Dell's jaws parted, his sharp fangs showing. Words tumbled from him, spoken in a language I didn't understand.

As soon as the words ended, pleasure filled me. I felt like I was getting high, the haze flowing through my veins.

"So this is magic?" I moaned, flexing my hips.

Dragons, magic, and sex— *oh my*! There had never been a better combination. All of the initial hesitation I'd had to being with these two had melted, replaced by the wonder of everything. Monsters or not, I was theirs.

His fingers suddenly weren't enough. I longed to be filled by something much, *much* bigger.

It didn't matter that his cock was as big as my leg at this point.

"Fill me," I gasped.

"You don't get to make commands," Dracon purred. He slipped another finger in, and I moaned as I pulsed around him.

I didn't care if I could walk tomorrow. I *needed* him inside of me.

Dracon let out a soft moan and pulled his hand free. He replaced it with the tip of his cock.

On a normal day, something that size would have made me scream. But I was wet and ready and now had a spell cast on me.

"I want all of you," I panted. "Every inch. Your knot—oh god!"

He thrust into me further. My body began to spasm, an orgasm crashing down on me without warning. I cried out, trying to take more of him.

His tail loosened as Dracon leaned forward, capturing my mouth with his. I wound my arms around him, breathing him in.

"You feel so good, my little kitten," he whispered, letting out a tight breath. "Are you going to keep being good for me?"

"Yes," I cried.

Every ridge that slipped in made me gasp until finally, I felt his knot at the opening. Tears slid down my cheeks, and my lips parted.

I had never been this full in my entire life. I looked down and gasped.

I could see the shape of him inside of me.

"I want your knot," I begged. I grabbed his face, bringing him back for another hungry kiss.

He was taking his time, but I wanted him to lose control with me like he had with Dell. I wanted him to fuck me just as hard.

"Not yet, kitten. You're not ready for my knot. Wrap your legs around me," he commanded.

I wanted to argue, but I did exactly as he said, rocking against him.

He let out a low growl and began to move, pumping in and out at a tantalizingly slow speed. Every movement was measured, everything was controlled.

It wasn't fair. One coffee date, and I had already sold my soul and body to two dragon shifters. This three day weekend was the beginning and the end for me, and damned if I wasn't excited about it.

I lost myself in the movements. No one had ever taken me like this, and the feeling of abandoning all thoughts and surrendering to primal lust was overwhelming. Dracon began to rut harder, drawing out screams from me as he took me.

His fingers slid between us, finding my clit. I came again, harder than any of the others, as soon as he touched it. I held onto him for dear life, my entire body riding the rollercoaster of heaven.

"God, you're so tight," he moaned, rutting into me harder. "I'm going to cum again, kitten."

I held onto him, and with one more thrust, he released. Heat filled me, his seed spilling out of me. I trembled, my muscles spasming as the two of us sank into the bed.

We laid there for a while until he moved, slowly pulling out of me.

My entire body shuddered. I was a mess, covered in all of our cum.

I couldn't move, but I didn't have to. Dell swooped in, his gigantic claws scooping me up. They were large enough that one set went around my chest and arms, and the other set went around my hips. The entire bed groaned as his dragon form moved the two of us.

He curled around me, letting out a noise of content. I had never been cuddled by a fucking mythological creature, and it was better than I could have ever imagined. I curled into his soft stomach. He rested his head next to me, letting out a sigh.

I raised my head, looking at Dracon.

He was watching the two of us with a satisfied smile.

"I'm going to go make some dinner," he said, rolling off the bed.

"How are you moving?" I groaned.

His laugh chimed through the room. "Both of you should rest. I'll let you know when dinner is ready."

With that, he disappeared.

I wanted to argue because I wanted him to join the two of us. But before I knew it, I was closing my eyes and falling asleep against Dell.

**DELL**

Dracon had fucked Kat and me within an inch of our lives, and what had been planned as dinner turned into brunch the next morning. Kat and I had slept through the night, eventually joined by a restless Dracon. I had offered to shift back, but he had been content lying next to my tail.

He had left us again a couple of hours ago, going downstairs to make the spaghetti we had planned to eat the night before.

I smiled, curling closer around Kat. Her breaths became softer as she fell asleep. Once the magic wore off, she would be sore— but then I'd run her a bubble bath. I'd pamper her and shower her in gifts.

She was mine. Just like Dracon was mine.

And I was theirs.

I let out another soft rumble. I hadn't been able to keep any other form after Dracon had taken me. My full dragon had taken over, and even now— I was still gathering the strength to change back.

It didn't matter. Kat was content, and I loved curling around her, protecting her. I rested my head next to her body, breathing in her scent.

She was perfect in every way. I studied her and couldn't help but feel a sense of pride. She was smart and sassy and beautiful. She had been so resistant to us but then had given in completely.

I owed the Barista everything now. He had given me not one but two mates. One that would submit to me and one that could dominate me.

I listened to the sounds of the kitchen below. I had always been alone in this house, and now that I wasn't— I finally felt happy. I had been alive for a few thousand years, and most I had spent...

What had I done? I had traveled the world. I had watched humanity grow and grow, pushing their old ways out and replacing them with new ones. They became smarter and harder. Their air became polluted, their cities became loud.

There had been a time when creatures had been widely accepted by humanity.

That was a thing of the past. We lived under their noses.

Well, most of them.

Kat was an exception, although her discovery of monsters had been tragic. It told me how open her heart was that she would ever consider being with one of us.

The world of monsters and humans was never supposed to collide. At least, that's what I had been taught. But over time, I had found that our two worlds *were* meant to overlap. Kat's soul fit with mine. She fit with Dracon's. I could feel it, the threads of fate binding our hearts together.

Then there was Dracon.

I knew most dragons in the world. Dragon shifters weren't all that common, and most of us knew the whereabouts of others. But he had come from nowhere.

What was his past? I wanted to know more about him.

Before Kat had arrived at Creature Cafe, we had talked for a while.

I now knew he had three roommates. Soon to be four, from the sounds of it.

He liked cooking, which was why he was downstairs. He had told me he was still trying to perfect his soup recipe — and when he spoke about it, his passion had been so intense.

He had grown up the same way I had. Alone. The difference was, he'd found other creatures and had befriended them. He told me about his minotaur friend Rum, and their ridiculous adventures. He told me about Dante, a hellish incubus that was someone he would trust his life with. Then he told me about other creatures through the world— ones that he could call up anytime and have a place to stay.

I had believed that all dragons were loners, but I had been wrong. Dracon had friends. He hadn't allowed the belief to define him.

Part of me envied him for that. But, I had the ability to change.

I would change now that I had Kat and Dracon. I would have them. I would make friends. I would stop being so alone.

Dracon wanted someone he could care for. That he could feed and make love to and nest with.

I wanted someone I could be with completely, fangs and all, that I could build a loving future with. I was tired of living in this world alone.

What did Kat want?

She stirred next to me, letting out the softest noise. I shifted my head and watched her wake up from her nap.

Her eyes met mine, and she beamed.

She had the brightest smile. All of the uneasiness that she had initially had melted away, revealing a jewel of a woman behind the shield.

"I dozed off," she whispered, slowly sitting up. She winced. "Oh fuck."

I let out a breath and then focused all of my energy. My body began to shrink, the bed becoming bigger as I morphed back into my most human form.

"Good morning," I said softly.

"Morning?" she asked with wide eyes.

"Closer to noon, actually. Dracon is making food."

I leaned into her, and we kissed. Her lips were already red and puffy from Dracon's love bites.

I drew back and winked at her. She blushed, her skin glowing.

"Let's get cleaned up. I think Dracon is almost finished with brunch," I said.

I picked her up and slid out of bed, carrying her to the door and out into the hall. Down at the end was another room— the enormous bathroom that had been built.

We went inside, and she gasped, her face lighting up.

"Holy shit, this place is beautiful."

"Can you stand for a moment?" I asked.

It was a genuine question, although it made her laugh. She began to move, and I slowly set her down. She held onto me for a moment, finding her balance.

"My legs feel like jello," she laughed. "You'll have to have the strongest bath salts in the world, or else I don't think it will help much."

"I'm a dragon, little kitten. I collect prizes in my travels. I have the *best* bath salts in the entire world."

Her eyes widened as I opened up a cabinet of all the soaps, bath bombs, bath salts, and oils a creature could dream of. There were things meant for Kat, things I might have gone out to buy from a few witches knowing she was visiting this weekend, and some things for Dracon and myself. Like the scale polish, the oil that turned hot, and the fang polishing salve.

Kat wobbled as she squeezed past me, letting out a tiny squeal. It made me unbelievably happy to see her smile.

Her excitement was contagious. I grinned as she reached into the massive cabinet and drew out a soft silk cloth and scale polish.

"Is this for you?" she asked, her gaze turning wicked.

I raised a brow. "Yes. Myself and Dracon. A dragon likes to care for their scales. This polish feels good and makes us shine. It's...an old sign of love. To be caressed by your partner in such a way...."

"I see," she said, smirking. "What about by a lover?"

"I'm supposed to be pampering you," I tutted, giving her ass a light pat. "Pick out your salts, and I'll run our bath."

Her cheeks were bright red as she turned back to the cabinet and carefully selected the ones she wanted. She went with a delicate jar of red salts, a blend of gardenia and dragons blood. I took it from her and then plucked a fresh soap bar out, one that was a deep black with gold swirls and flecks.

I went to the massive bathtub and reached in, turning on the water. It started to pool, and I dumped the salts in.

Kat came up behind me, her finger tracing down my spine.

I shuddered, closing my eyes for just a moment as the sound of water rushing filled the room.

"I want to see your wings again. They were beautiful."

I was frozen in place, the desire to take her hard building up in me. "Kat," I whispered.

Her fingers danced on my shoulder blades. "Please," she pouted.

I sighed and let them shift out. I felt them unfurl, releasing the softest moan as the pressure of holding the human form melted just a little.

"Why do you force yourself into that other form if it bothers you? Your wings are beautiful," she said as she moved around to look at them. Her hands reached out, caressing the iridescent webbing.

I straightened and looked down at her, studying her. "You're a human. I don't want to scare you."

I wasn't trying to ruin the mood, but I couldn't fight the insecurities rising up.

"Most humans would try to kill me. Wings? Scales? I'm a *monster*."

"You're not," she whispered, her brows pulling together. "Dell, you're beautiful. You're what girls dream of."

I snorted. "I doubt that, kitten."

"Okay, well, you obviously have never been on the internet. And regardless, I think you're beautiful," she said, crossing her arms.

She was so tiny and now a bit angry, which made me chuckle.

I leaned in, pausing before I touched her ear. "You're telling me you aren't scared? Even just a little?"

I could hear her heartbeat picking up. Her blood was

racing in her veins, the scent of her arousal becoming stronger and stronger.

"I have sharp teeth," I growled.

"The better to eat me with," she whispered.

"A tail."

"Perfect for riding," she said, swallowing hard.

"I have talons that could rip apart metal," I said, piercing her nipple with one of them.

"Fuck," she gasped. I caught her as she stumbled into me and lifted her. "Better to...ahhh, shit," she cried.

I took her nipple into my mouth and sucked, her blood filling my mouth. I then healed up the wound and drew back, looking deep into her eyes.

"You really think you can handle us monsters, little kitten?"

"You're not the only one with claws," she growled, glaring at me.

Before she could pull out of my grip, I lifted her up and threw her over my shoulder. She let out a squeal as I stepped into the bathtub. Steam rose up around us as I sank into the water and then settled her between my legs.

She moaned as soon as the water hit her skin. The salts would sting a little in certain areas, but it would help her relax and recover for what Dracon and I had in store for her later.

I feared that she would run from me. I feared that she wouldn't accept me.

Now that I had tasted her, that I had tasted Dracon, I feared even more.

What if I ended up alone again?

She leaned against my chest, her head falling back against me. I held onto her as the water continued to fill the bath, easing my own body as well.

Dracon hadn't been easy on me. I hadn't wanted him to be. There were other things, other dark fantasies that I wanted to explore...

"This feels so good, Dell," she moaned.

I stiffened, my cock hardening from her voice. She tipped her head back until she could look up at me, and then she smirked.

"Are you really just going to sit there and look pretty?"

I let out a growl. Those would be her famous last words.

## Dracon

I heard a scream from upstairs, and my blood turned cold. I turned off the stove and ran, practically flying up the stairs and down the hall.

The sound of water splashing drew me towards a door and I kicked it open, stepping in.

Steam billowed through the entire room. There was another scream, but this time I recognized it was edged in pleasure and not...my nightmares. I stopped, focusing my gaze.

Dell and Kat were joined together, their heavy pants making me go hard. I went towards the tub and looked down at the two of them, raising a brow.

Kat let out another moan, her head pressed against his chest. She hadn't even heard me come in. Her eyes were heavily lidded, her pink lips parted.

Dell let out a soft growl.

I looked down and scowled.

"You knotted her?!" I asked, exasperated.

"She teased me," he moaned, tipping his head back.

He tried to move, and she let out another scream.

I couldn't help it. I laughed, clutching my stomach for just a moment. All of the fear I had felt had been pointless. Had I really thought Dell had hurt her? "I told you," I said, kneeling down to the floor. I reached out, placing my hand on her lower back.

"It's...it's so much," she gasped. She was melted against Dell, her muscles twitching.

I reached over to the faucet and turned off the rushing water. Serenity surrounded us, only interrupted by the softening purrs coming from Dell.

My cock began to strain against my pants. Seeing the two of them joined this way and knowing what it meant...

"I thought the two of you were sleeping," I teased, resting my palm back on her. She let out the cutest mewl but then started to try and move. "No, no, no. Don't move, kitten. His knot will get bigger before you can move."

"Bigger?" she squeaked.

"Yes," I chuckled, leaning over the edge of the tub. I reached down and ran my finger across his balls.

He moaned, his muscles tensing as he did his best to not jerk. "Dracon," he gasped. "Fuck. Kat, you feel so good."

"You're still cumming," she whispered breathlessly, "How are you still cumming?"

"I told you that you weren't ready for a knot," I said, but I smirked. The only sparks in my heart were ones of absolute excitement. I licked my lips, studying how wide his knot had spread her. "He's going to keep filling you until he literally can't anymore. How do you feel?"

"Good," she rasped. Her cheeks were bright pink, her lips still parted. "I've never...Ahhh." She suddenly arched, and I watched as her entire body spasmed, an orgasm taking her. "I can't stop," she cried.

Dell watched her in reverie, his green eyes filled with affection and amazement.

Before her orgasm finished, I shifted enough to be able to lift the two of them together from the tub. Neither one of them fought me. I shook my head and carried them downstairs. "I can't have the two of you turning into raisins. You're going to stay knotted on the couch where I can keep you in my sights."

Once I got into the living room, I slowly rolled them onto the cushion. Dell ended up on top with a heavy groan, his hips moving just a little. Kat cried out, her nails raking down his back. I watched angry red streaks ignite across his skin and licked my lips.

I knelt down again next to them, and this time, I took Dell's face into my hand. He leaned in for a kiss, his mouth ravaging mine. I ruffled his sandy hair, reveling in his purr.

"You're going to end up in heat now," I whispered to him. "And so will she. I won't be able to control myself."

Despite all the excitement I felt, I knew that the entire weekend had just changed.

I was a dominant dragon. An alpha. I would never submit to another. When I knotted with my mate, they would take it, and their body would go into heat. It was chemical, magical, and completely ignorant to whatever else was going on in someones life. The three of us could be in the middle of a battle, and if I'd knotted one and triggered the heat...

Well, I'd be fucking them both non stop.

Dell wasn't an alpha dragon. He was an omega. In the world of dragons, that meant a couple of things. One, his knot would trigger heat too. The difference was, he would want to be bred. Over and over again. Given that we had a third, he would want to fuck her too until his body was convinced she carried his young.

And now that he had knotted with Kat, it would not only send him into a frenzied heat— our little human would go into one too.

All of the careful ropes I had put up this weekend, all of the boundaries, all of the trying to be a gentleman— all of it would be off the table now.

"I'm sorry," he gasped. "I'm sorry. I didn't think this through."

Kat surprised both of us by reaching up and grabbing his face. "Do NOT apologize for this," she growled. "I've never felt like this in my entire life. I'm—" Her words were drowned by another orgasm. Her entire body arched, and she yelled, lost in the euphoric pleasure overtaking her. "AGAIN?" she wailed. Tears streaked out of the corner of her eyes as her face lit up with pleasure.

I watched her, my cock now begging to be touched. I wished that I was the one buried inside of her, but I knew it was only a matter of time.

Better to take his knot first. Mine would be even bigger.

"How long does this last?" she moaned.

I snorted. "You have at least another hour to go and several more orgasms. And then, you'll eat dinner. By the end of dinner, you'll be begging to be knotted again. You're about to be almost nothing more than my sex slave. Same for Dell, too. But don't worry," I said, standing up. "I'll take care of both of you. Enjoy the ride, kitten. I'm going to go finish the spaghetti."

I grinned and left the two of them on the couch. I went back to the kitchen, back to the stove.

I was preparing two variations for spaghetti. One for Kat, since she was a human, and one for myself and Dell.

I stared at the pots and scowled.

Which one was which?

Fuck.

I turned the stove back on and glared as the heat came back to life. The silver pots started burbling again. I still had vegetables thrown out onto the counter and raw meatballs waiting to be cooked. Beef, lamb, and then a sustainably sourced slab of demon meat.

Dante was my go-to for such meats. He liked his steaks raw and hellish. Rum wasn't a fan of demon meat, but I really liked how it tasted. I was sure Dell would enjoy it too.

I sank back into the rhythm again, still listening to Dell and Kat's occasional groans. Their scents were strong enough that not even the spaghetti sauce could mask them.

It made my mouth water. Maybe I'd be finished cooking just in time for him to pull out of her so I could go lap everything up...

"Draconnnn."

I raised both of my eyebrows as Kat's moan echoed from the living room. I paused from cooking for a moment and then frowned.

She probably needed water.

Hell, Dell probably did too.

I should have made them both eat last night, but I hadn't the heart to wake them. Now, it was past noon, and my two mates hadn't eaten or drunk anything.

I scooped up all the vegetables and tossed them into the sauce pots, rinsed my hands in the marble sink, and then plucked glasses from one of the cabinets.

It hadn't taken me long to feel at home in Dell's kitchen.

He seemed to have never used it, but it still had everything I could ever need to cook a full course meal. I could even run my own shop out of here.

I paused for a moment. That was the dream.

My heart warmed a little, and I went to the fridge, filling their cups with ice. I grabbed a lemon from a fruit basket and used my talon to cut into it, squeezing some juice in before adding water.

I then went out to the living room. Slivers of light slid through the tightly drawn curtains, escaping here and there from their restraints. The two of them were a pretty picture, their sweet-smelling bodies paired together.

"How am I supposed to cook a meal when I have two delicious snacks tempting me?" I asked.

Kat let out a small giggle, and Dell raised his head. They were still knotted, but it was finally beginning to come down.

"Here," I said, standing over both of them. "Drink up, you dehydrated bitches."

I helped both of them drink their water. Dell drained his, and when Kat tried to stop halfway, I shook my head.

"All of it."

She sighed dramatically but then drank the rest, making a face at me at the end.

"Alright. Ready to pull out?" I asked Dell.

"It's a little late for that," Kat giggled.

Dell laughed, but then it slid into a moan. "Are you ready, baby?"

Kat nodded, her eyes going wide.

I licked my lips and went to the floor, wanting to watch them untie. Kat began to writhe, but Dell grabbed both of her wrists, pinning them above her head.

"Be still, kitten," he whispered.

He slowly began to pull out. I watched gleefully as his cock sprang free, and the cum began to flow out like milk. Before she could make a noise, I spun her to the edge and held the cup up to the cum dripping from her.

"Oh my god," she whispered.

"I want a taste," I said, pulling the glass away.

Her lips parted, her eyes widening in shock as I held it to my lips. My forked tongue flicked out, and I licked the edge of the glass.

My cock was pulsing now, begging to be free.

I tipped the glass back, and their cum poured in. It was the sweetest cocktail. Like a sex-flavored margarita with a salted rim.

I drank every drop and let out a moan. Kat leaned forward and grabbed my face. "I want a taste," she demanded, bringing me in for a kiss.

It was going to take every ounce of control for me to make it through our meal.

**KAT**

I had finished my bath and changed into a fresh set of clothes before heading back down for lunch. I was walking like a damn cowboy to a showdown. My knees wobbled with every step, but I still took them, refusing to let Dracon or Dell carry me.

Never in my entire life had I ever been twisted up the way these two had twisted me.

I lingered on the bottom step of the staircase for a moment, staring at the front door.

We were only on day two of our three-day weekend, and I was falling apart. Willing to throw my entire heart at the two of them.

The two dragons had turned me into putty.

Dell's moment of soft fear had tugged on my heart-strings. And Dracon...the dirty dragon had a hotline straight to my vagina's deepest darkest fantasies.

The Barista hadn't been wrong, which made me just a

bit sour. Not because I wanted him to be wrong. All week, I had been anticipating these three days. Every morning, I had woken up panting from the ridiculously hot dreams that had plagued me.

Dracon and Dell. Dell and Dracon. The two dragons had burned their way into my soul.

I just...never thought I'd be able to be with someone again.

Cal's death had truly shaken me. It had turned me upside down. I had become a creature of depression, barely able to crawl out of my apartment.

The coffee shop had saved me.

The Barista had saved me.

And here he was again, saving all three of us.

The only problem was the fear niggling at me in the back of my head.

What if they turned into monsters?

What if they found out about Cal and hated me for it?

What if the werewolf that had slaughtered him found out about us?

Everyone had their deep dark secrets. But not everyone's deep dark secrets involved a psychotic creature.

The Barista had friends in low *and* high places. He was known for protecting the innocents from monsters, and I was just another human in the line of humans he had kept from death's greedy hands.

Sometimes it made me wonder about him. Why did he think he had to save everyone and help them find love?

I'd never asked him, but then again— I wasn't his therapist.

Either way, all of the fears eating at me were ugly. And acidic.

I couldn't let the past cannibalize my future.

I snapped out of my thoughts and stepped into the living room, following the glorious scent to the kitchen.

Dracon stood over the stove, an apron tied around his taut waist. He was shirtless and wearing black jeans. His skin glistened with dark blue scales, his back muscles rippling as he stirred a pot.

Dell was standing next to him with a frown. "I don't know, Dracon. Which one is hers? It's kind of important."

"Hush. I think it's this one. Here, try it," Dracon said quickly, holding out a spoon to Dell.

Dell snorted and then tasted the sauce. He frowned. "Hmmm...let me try the other one."

Dracon held up a different spoon for Dell to try.

"They taste...how can they possibly taste the same if one of them has demon meat and the other doesn't?"

"Well," Dracon said, a bit frustrated, "Everyone *knows* that demon meat can taste like lamb. If I hadn't gotten distracted, it wouldn't have been a problem."

Dell ginned like a boy. "Oh, come on, man. It was a good distraction."

"It was a perfect one, but now my spaghetti is questionable," Dracon grumbled.

That was my cue to make my entrance. Dell's gaze met mine as I stepped into the kitchen, and I felt my pussy squeeze all over again. My stomach did a slow roll.

"You smell good," he said, his eyes turning almost black.

Dracon turned around, his honey gaze darkening as well.

Uh oh. I was being looked at like dinner by two sexy dragons.

I raised a brow. "Can humans eat demon meat?"

"NO," they both said together.

I laughed and moved further into the massive kitchen.

Everything about Dell's home was modern and luxurious, including the marble counters, sink, and stainless steel appliances. There was a breakfast nook to the right that could seat the three of us. The windows had blinds that were pulled tight, but I wanted to let some of the light in.

I listened to Dracon and Dell go back and forth about the pasta as I slid into the cushioned seat of the breakfast nook. I reached for the blinds and gave them a tug.

They folded up and revealed my worst nightmare.

My scream tore through the room, and I fell back, my butt hitting the floor. Dracon and Dell were on me within the second, but I couldn't pry my eyes away from the window.

It had been him.

It had been the wolf. Watching. On the other side.

How...? How? Nothing made sense. The bastard was supposed to be in Alaska— far, far away from me.

"Kat!!" Dracon thundered.

I realized that they were both talking to me, their hulking forms surrounding me.

"KAT!" Dracon yelled again.

I blinked and looked up at him.

Dell muttered something under his breath and stood, moving out of the kitchen towards the front of the house.

"No!" I squealed, scrambling up. Dracon caught me before I could run. I heard the front door start to open and screamed again. "Stop! Stop! *DELL!*"

He didn't listen. The door opened, and I heard it slam shut, a roar echoing.

"Baby," Dracon whispered. "Whatever you saw, one of us has to investigate."

"No," I cried. Tears were streaming down my cheeks

now, my heart racing. "No. He'll kill him. He's here. I don't know how. I don't...."

This was my nightmare.

I lifted my fingers to my face and pinched my cheek until I felt blood vessels threatening to pop. Dracon slapped my hand away and scooped me up, holding me against his chest.

"Breath, little kitten. Whatever monster is out there, they are no match for two dragon shifters. I will slaughter them before they ever touch you."

He didn't understand. He didn't know. He didn't know anything.

He also wouldn't let me go.

I began to cry harder and gave up on trying to roll out of his burly arms.

I heard the door open and slam closed again.

Dell came back into the kitchen and stood in the doorway, staring at the two of us. He scratched the back of his head. "There...Kat, there wasn't anything out there."

"He was there," I said. I then scowled.

This time, Dracon let me stand. I wobbled for a moment, still made of jello from all of the orgasms, and then crossed my arms.

"I'm not crazy. He was there."

"*Who* was?" Dracon asked.

I wasn't crazy. My mind began to race. I had seen the bright yellow eyes.

"The werewolf," I said, fighting all of the doubts beginning to rise up.

Dell started to say something, but Dracon silenced him with a look.

"I'm not crazy!" I yelled, throwing my hand out. "I saw him! My fucking husband's murderer!"

Silence settled between all three of us.

"*Husband?*" Dracon snarled.

My entire heart dropped. My eyes fell to the floor, tears blurring my vision.

I had done it.

I had fucked everything up. Just like I had feared.

"You didn't tell us that you're married," Dell said coldly.

More tears fell. I couldn't think of what to say.

"*Speak!*" Dracon barked.

His fury was beginning to swell in the room, a low growl rumbling in his chest.

"God damn it, *human,* I told you to speak!"

That was the end of the fuse for both of us.

There were three things Mr. Dragon-Bastard didn't know about me.

One, I refused to be degraded as human.

Two, I wasn't going to be commanded like a dog.

Three, I knew kung fu.

**DELL**

Before I could intercept them, Kat threw herself at Dracon like a rabid chihuahua. It was like watching a disaster in slow motion, and there was nothing I could do about it.

She didn't know that Dracon's last thread of control had just snapped.

She hit him— but she didn't hit *him*.

She hit his snout as his body burst into a massive dragon.

I lunged across the kitchen and grabbed Kat, yanking her back into the living room as Dracon filled the entire kitchen. The entire house shook as he roared, his teeth snapping together.

"Fuck!" she squealed.

I gritted my teeth and scooped her up. I was about to run, but Dracon had shoved himself into the living room, and the tip of his tail had twisted around my legs.

"God damn it," I growled. I threw Kat towards the edge of the living room just as I fell.

Dracon's piercing roar filled the house again. His tail rolled me over onto my back, his teeth baring at me. Globs of saliva dripped onto my face.

"Dell!

I arched to look at her and said as calmly as I could, "Hey kitten, you need to run and hide now."

Before she could say anything, Dracon's hot jaws opened and he snapped me up into his mouth.

The bastard seriously needed a breath mint.

His jaws clamped around me, and I went still, trying not to squirm too much. It was instinct to try to fight out, but if I did that— his dragon would just swallow me.

I could hear Kat screaming on the other side.

This evening had really gone south.

Kat had a husband? And there was a wolf out to get her?

I hadn't smelled anything outside. That didn't mean she was lying, though.

Maybe...fuck. I didn't even know. Maybe the scent of our heat had distracted me.

I closed my eyes, and I couldn't help myself.

I let out a moan.

His tongue was...

Fuck, I was just laying on his tongue.

My cock was starting to pulse in my pants.

The heat was beginning to take over me again. Dracon had been right.

Knotting with her had unlocked a whole slew of potential problems. Ones that we had wanted to wait to deal with until our relationships were all built.

Dracon's need to protect us would drive him over the

edge once he became himself again. He would never forgive himself for eating me, although I'd have to convince him that I wasn't...

I wasn't against it.

That secretly...

*I'd always wanted to know.*

I let out another huff again, my hands sliding down to my cock. The movement made his tongue shift, moving me with it. Another low growl rumbled through him.

I strained my hearing for a moment, listening for Kat.

She wasn't screaming anymore.

In fact, I could hear her moaning.

"What's wrong with me?" I heard her cry.

I squeezed my eyes shut. Dracon had timed dinner so that we'd be able to eat before succumbing to passion again.

Well, the spaghetti was off the table now. I was what was for dinner, along with Kat, more than likely.

My entire body was wet now.

I gripped my cock through my pants and moaned.

I needed to cum. *Now.*

His tongue suddenly rolled me against the side of his fangs. I used the motion to help me wiggle my pants partly down, just enough to free my cock.

"Fuck. Dracon," I gasped, thrusting my hips.

My cock rubbed against one of his fangs. I began to thrust, unable to stop myself.

The frenzy was starting.

My nerves were burning, my balls begging to be touched. I felt like I was on fire and the only thing in the world that could douse the flames was sex.

"God," I groaned. I reached under my shirt and began to play with my nipples while humping him.

Could he feel me? Did he know the things I was doing inside of his mouth?

Before I knew it, all of my clothes had been stripped free. He could swallow me if he wanted. At this point, I didn't care.

I wiggled until I was able to roll over onto my stomach, and then I started fucking his tongue as hard as I could.

I had to cum.

I was coated in his saliva now, my skin slick. I moaned again and felt the build up— it was excruciating.

"Fuck!" I yelled.

One more thrust and my cock came harder than it had earlier with Kat. I cried out, emptying out onto Dracon's massive tongue.

A low growl surrounded me and his jaws suddenly opened. I was rolled out, my body hitting the floor.

I was panting, the cool air of the living room hitting me.

"Dell!" Kat gasped.

I cracked open one eye just as Kat threw herself on me. Her expression was one of confusion.

"Why are you naked?"

Dracon's low rumble made us both look up. He slowly began to morph back into his normal state.

So the cum had done it, huh? Cured his fucking temper tantrum.

I let out a breathless laugh.

The weekend suddenly felt like an eternity. At this rate, we would all fall apart at some point.

I had a lot of questions for Kat. A lot of questions for Dracon.

A lot of questions for myself and the fact that I just got off to the idea of being eaten by Dracon.

"Fuck," Dracon gasped, collapsing to the floor next to

us. His chest was heaving, his skin hot. "I'm so sorry. *Fuck*," he said again.

"I'm sorry too," Kat whispered, tears streaking down her cheeks. Her hair was a mess around her face, the golden curls sticking to her.

I reached for her and slid her over my body, laying her between Dracon and me. The three of us laid there for a while, silence settling between us.

Suddenly, Kat let out a hysteric laugh. Her giggle was contagious, forcing me to grin. "Well," Kat finally said. "Today has gone to hell."

"A little bit," Dracon groaned. "Dell, why do I taste your cum in my mouth?"

Heat bloomed in my cheeks. "Uh..."

He sat up, looking over Kat at me. He raised a dark brow, his golden eyes glimmering.

Oh, he knew EXACTLY why.

Bastard.

Kat looked from him to me and then back again. "Maybe we should order pizza, and all try to sit down. I came again, and that seems to have...forced whatever hell-fire that has consumed my lady bits to chill out."

"It's temporary," Dracon chuckled. "But yes. And then you can explain your husband to us."

Kat's eyes flickered, her grin dying. She nodded, mournful. "I'm sorry to both of you. He's dead, so...." She trailed off for a moment and the took in a quick breath. "I rather explain now, if you're willing to listen."

"We are," I answered, glancing at Dracon. His golden eyes had narrowed, his lips drawing into a thin line.

"We were high school sweethearts," she said softly. I watched the way her eyes watered, breaking my heart. I didn't want to see her cry. "He was my best friend. We did everything together. He was my first for everything. My first kiss, my first time, my first love, my first marriage. I'm not sure exactly how it happened, my memories are fuzzy. But there was a night that we were camping outside of the city. A fun weekend trip to get away. I was setting up the fire when I heard a rustle in the trees. I thought it was Cal coming back, but it wasn't. It was a massive werewolf with eyes that burned straight into me. He had blood on his face. That's when I realized he had something in his mouth..." She sucked in another breath. I could hear her heart racing.

Dracon lifted his hand and slid it over her stomach, spreading his fingers across her torso to calm her.

"It was Cal," she whispered. "It was his head. I screamed and ran. I don't remember what happened after that, but I woke up in a cabin. The Barista was there." She smiled, relaxing a little. "He helped me. He helped me heal. And he promised to protect me. He's the only person that could ever convince me to go on a date with two men, you know?"

I chuckled, the humor easing the tension.

My heart ached for her, and I tried not to wince at the rush of relief I felt. There was a little part of me that wondered if Dracon and I could create 'firsts' for her too.

I reached out and grabbed her chin, pulling her in for a kiss. She melted just a little, breathing me in.

Dracon sat up, pulling his hand away. He was quiet for a moment and then nodded. "I'll order the pizza," Dracon said, rolling to his feet.

The two of us watched him head for the kitchen.

"He hates me," she whispered.

I shook my head, forcing her to look at me. "Far far from it, kitten. Today has just been insane. But he doesn't hate you. You scared us both."

Her eyes filled with tears. "I'm sorry...."

"Kat, stop. First, thank you for sharing with us about Cal. Dragons are extremely possessive so the idea of you belonging to another triggered that. I can't speak for Dracon entirely, but I can say— knowing the story has helped douse any flames of jealousy. And I haven't stopped loving you one bit just because your secret was revealed."

We both stopped, and my eyes widened just a little.

Love.

I'd really gone off the deep end, hadn't I?

The heat in my cheeks turned to a flame, but that didn't stop Kat from cupping my face and bringing me in for another sweet kiss.

"We're all three a little crazy, aren't we?" she whispered.

I smiled and nodded. "Yes, but I wouldn't want it any other way."

**DRAGON**

I snatched my phone off the floor and wiped the tomato sauce off with a random towel. The kitchen was an absolute disaster. It looked like a crime scene with all of the white marble splattered with spaghetti sauce.

I could hear Dell and Kat talking to each other. My heart gave a dark little tug. He was convincing her that she probably hadn't seen anything outside, and she seemed to be agreeing to it.

He said he hadn't smelled any other scent, but that didn't mean a werewolf wasn't out there.

I had fucked up. I had lost my temper, and I could have killed Kat. Dell would have been fine... but, Kat was a human.

Now that my phone was clean, I opened it up to text Dante.

**My human also has a stalker, apparently.**

The typing bubble popped up almost immediately, which told me that it was Peter. Not Dante.

Peter was Dante's human mate— the love of his life.

**Dante (aka Peter): Hi Dracon! Dante gave me permission to text you since he is busy. Is your human okay? Maybe all of you should come here. I'm almost out of soup, and I'm craving it. I know Rum misses you.**

I snorted. Rum probably did miss me, but then again— he was probably in the middle of another painting and had forgotten what day it was. My minotaur friend was always off painting unless he was eating my food.

Peter had grown on me significantly. I wasn't as close with him, but I did think of him as under my protection. And, one of his pregnancy cravings was the soup I made. I'd left him with an entire vat of it, so he should have been set.

Dante would have to cook some then. I grinned at the thought of my red-tailed devil of a friend in an apron.

Hell, he'd changed me too. I'd never forget how undone my ancient incubus friend had become when he met Peter.

That was happening to me now. Except it wasn't one love, it was two.

**Sorry, Peter. We're staying here. Have Dante text me when he's available. I'm going to call the Barista.**

**D/P: Okay! If anything happens, let us know. Rum says he will throw hands.**

I snorted again. Part of me wondered why Dante hadn't texted me, but the bastard wouldn't unless I really needed him. He wasn't a fan of cell phones.

I pulled up the Barista's contact and clicked to call. It rang twice, and then I was greeted by an angry man.

"WHO IS THIS?" the Barista's gruff voice growled. "How the fuck did you get this—"

"Barista, it's Dracon," I snapped quietly.

"Oh." I could almost hear him find his composure. "Hi, Dracon. I thought you were with Kat and Dell this weekend."

"I am," I said, fighting the temper that was rising up again. "And we ran into a problem. She thinks she saw a werewolf? One that fucking *ate* her *husband* years ago? Ring a bell, you fucking coffee bean cupid?"

I was met with a few moments of quiet.

"Where are the three of you now?" he asked darkly.

"At Dell's. Does this normally happen to the couples you put together? Psychopaths finding out and trying to attack them?"

"No," he said. There was a hint of hesitation, the kind that made me feel uneasy. "No, it's not normal. Did the wolf attack you?"

"No, but Kat swears that she saw him outside. Dell couldn't scent him, but I'm still concerned. I need to know what we're up against, Barista. Also, what the fuck is going on? Who did you piss off? And why didn't you kill the fucker years ago?"

"I'm sure it's just a coincidence," he answered. "This has never been a problem before. But, of course, both Peter and Kat have come from dark situations. And you know how monsters are, Dracon."

True. I didn't buy it, but he wasn't wrong.

"Are we in danger?" I asked, drumming my fingers on the countertop.

"If it's truly the werewolf that ate her husband, then yes. Well, she's in danger. You and Dell are probably not. But I wouldn't let her out of your sights. I can send a couple of friends to hunt him."

'Friends'.

"I wouldn't mind the extra security. We'll also put Kat to sleep and then check the area. Barista..." I trailed off, wondering where the line was when talking to this man. Creature. Soul? "I already killed someone recently because of humans with monsters hunting them. I didn't mind, the vampire was evil. But..."

"I'm going to do some research, Dracon. I apologize that the wolf went after her, but I can't control every-thing. I've had her under my protection for years now, and it makes sense that the moment she goes under someone else's— he attacks. He ate her husband but...he was never imprisoned. There were some parts to that situ-ation that weren't clear. It was deemed self-defense. Kat doesn't know everything about it, and it should stay that way."

I mulled over his words, my wheels turning.

I didn't need to know everything, but the thought of Kat being kept in the dark made my gut twist a little.

But, sometimes, ignorance was bliss.

"Okay," I breathed out.

"If you need me, holler. I'll send Al and Jasper. They'll be there soon. Al is a werewolf, but he's one of the good ones."

"Wouldn't expect less of someone you call a friend," I said.

The Barista made a grumbling noise. "One last thing, Dracon."

"Yes?"

"The wolf wouldn't be out to kill her. He'd be out to take her as a mate. Those years ago, he was convinced she belonged to him and no-one else."

I growled, rage burning in my throat. "If I find him, he's dead."

"Agreed."

With that, I hung up. I stared at the counter for a moment, my thoughts still turning. I picked up the phone again and ordered pizza, barely paying attention as I ordered five pepperoni, three cheese with jalapeño, and then one with pineapple and anchovies.

The human on the other end was extremely confused by my order, but I didn't care. I finished the order and hung up.

At least now we'd all be able to eat. The kitchen was a disaster and would be a bitch to clean.

I wanted to check the perimeter myself.

I'd do it, then we'd lock down the house.

Pizza, perimeter, lockdown.

Then I could focus on their heat.

My mouth instantly watered, and I groaned.

"Dracon?"

I turned around. Kat was standing in the doorway, watching me carefully.

We stared at each other for what felt like eons.

I had almost eaten her.

My heart thumped, harder and harder.

How was I supposed to protect her from creatures when I was just as bad as all of them?

Dell's voice rang through my mind, echoing through the

bond I had given him. *She's all yours. I'm going to go scout outside again.*

*Barista said he's sending friends. I don't know when they'll be here.*

*They're already here,* Dell answered.

I scowled. The Barista was quick.

*I need to know if what she saw was really that wolf,* Dell said.

*Let me know.* A pang of guilt and worry went through me, but I felt his response to it.

*Don't worry about me. She needs you right now, and you need her. I need to know that the wolf is gone.*

His voice then left me, but I knew I could reach him if I needed to.

Kat crossed the room, sliding her body up next to mine. Her expression was one of concern, her brows drawn together.

I pulled her closer and leaned in, breathing in her scent. She smelled delicious and perfect and...

"I'm sorry," we both said simultaneously.

I let out a dark chuckle and swept her up, holding her in a hug. She clung to me, burying her face at the base of my neck.

"You smell nice," she whispered.

I shivered, closing my eyes for a moment.

"You smell like you...."

"Need you," she breathed, suckling at my neck.

"Baby," I gasped.

Her little mouth clamped onto me, and my knees nearly buckled. All of the rage and worry turned to primal urges. I wanted to fuck her, here and now.

She kept sucking, kissing up and down my neck. She leaned up, her teeth biting my ear.

I gasped again, letting out a moan.

"Careful," I groaned. "You'll bond us."

"Bond?" she murmured.

She went back in and bit even harder. I spun her around and sat her on the kitchen counter, planting my hands on either side of her.

"Yes," I rasped. My throat was dry, aching to be quenched by her taste. "Little human, you don't know anything about dragons— do you?"

"Dell told me that you bonded him to you," she said, running her pink tongue across her lips. "He told me that when you bite someone, you can tie your souls together because of the magic."

My eyes narrowed.

Her lips curved up into a smile. "I want one."

I blew out a breath. Her innocence weakened me. "Kat, it's not just...."

She arched her head, exposing her slender throat to me.

My heart damn near stopped. I let out a low snarl.

"I want you. I want you to bond me and knot me. To breed me. I want you to fill me up with—"

My hand went around her throat, cutting off her words. Her eyes widened, her breath catching.

"You want to be my little slut?" I growled mercilessly.

"Ye—yes," she choked out.

I tightened my grip a little, enjoying the way her cheeks turned red.

"You don't want me to bond you. I have dark desires, Kat. Too much for you." I eased up the pressure, allowing her to breathe.

The possessive streak was rearing its ugly head, and there was nothing I could do to stop it. I wanted to control her. I wanted to control the air she breathed.

She had woken the dragon within me. The primal, dark side that had been buried for ages.

"But not too dark for Dell? That isn't fair. What do you want to do to me? Eat me? Cut me? Choke me? Spank me?"

I tightened my grip again and bared my teeth at her. "You're a little brat. You think you're so strong, but I could snap you in two. Your bones would become powder under my jaws. I could rip you in half just with the full size of my dragon cock."

Her eyes were blazing now— burning with delight, a hint of fear, and unbridled lust.

"Do it," she gasped.

There was a knife on the counter from when I had been prepping dinner. I snatched it up with my other hand and replaced the one choking her with its sharp edge.

"You're trying to push me," I snarled.

"Yes. I want to see you lose control again. You're like Dell. Both of you are so used to hiding from humans. So used to having to be *good* creatures."

"And what about you, Kat? You're hiding things too," I snapped, pressing the blade in further. A little drop of blood bloomed as her skin opened a little.

"I'm not hiding who I am. I'm hiding my past because I don't even want to face it. I should have told you about Cal, and I will. But I'm not here hiding who I am," she said. She leaned into the knife more, her gaze now filled with a fire I'd never forget. "I like a little pain with my pleasure, Dracon. I like to give control."

"You're a little crazy," I said. "But I think I love that about you."

She grinned, and with that— our dynamics shifted. I was her alpha ,and she would submit to me however I saw fit. I would dominate her until every piece of her soul belonged to me.

I wound a fist in her hair and dragged her off the counter. She yelped as I walked her across the kitchen to the breakfast table. I shoved her towards it.

"Bend over," I barked. "And once you're in position, you better not move an inch, or I'll mark your pretty skin."

She moaned as she bent over the table, giving me a perfect view of her ass and dripping pussy. I licked my lips, her scent filling the air.

I stepped up right behind her and traced a finger from her spine, between her ass cheeks, and then to her entrance. I eased in a finger, listening to the way her breath hitched.

She was so wet. So wet for me.

I lifted the knife and traced her skin. She shivered beneath me, her muscles twitching.

"Not an inch, princess," I whispered.

I replaced the one finger inside of her with two. I began to slowly fuck her with them, still tracing lines over her back. The blade hadn't broken skin yet, just a taste of what I was going to do to her.

"Tell me, little kitten," I said, looking down at her. "Are you sure you want this? That you want both of us? That you want me?"

"Yes," she gasped. "Yes. I didn't think I did at first. And I still...I don't want to ruin anything."

I shoved three fingers in her, and she jerked. The edge of the knife nicked her, and I hissed. "Bad girl," I growled, withdrawing my fingers.

"No!" I gasped. "Please give them back. *Fuck.*"

"You're so scared of ruining everything, aren't you?" I asked.

"Dracon," she pleaded.

"Beg."

"Please," she cried.

"Is that all you can do?" I asked darkly. "*Please, Dracon*," I mimicked. "You sound like a stupid little human. You'll never get my knot this way."

**KAT**

I'd said to myself that I'd never take being degraded as a human, but now I was practically eating out of Dracon's hands.

If he told me to bend over, I'd bend over.

If he told me to crawl, I'd crawl.

His tongue slipped inside of me, and I dug my nails into the surface of the table.

This was torture. I wasn't allowed to move, and he was doing everything in his power to make me squirm. Every time he won, I was spanked. Or he'd draw a little cut across my back, lick up the blood, and heal the wound with his fiery dragon magic.

Pain and pleasure had become synonymous.

I wanted his knot. I wanted him to be buried inside of me the same way that Dell had been. I ached for the fullness, to be completely taken.

He coaxed another orgasm out of me, and my voice was

hoarse as I cried out. It crashed into me, a wave of euphoria and heat electrifying my veins.

I felt the tip of his cock brush against me, and my eyes flew open, anticipation pulsing through me.

"Please," I begged.

"No," he answered, still just hovering.

He was testing me. I could lean back and sheathe myself on him.

I wanted to. To risk more punishment.

But I wanted him to give me his knot.

"Please," I whispered, letting out a soft whimper. "Please. Give me your knot. Your bond. I need them."

"No. Only good girls get those things, and you haven't been good."

My heart began to hammer, my entire body burning with desire. I had just cum, but my brain was being clouded with lust again.

"Dracon," I whispered.

His scaled hand smacked my ass hard. The sound of it against my skin cracked through the air, my yelp following after it.

Suddenly, I felt the tip of his tail wrapping around my leg, spreading me further. The scales were warm against my skin, the spikes tickling my other thigh.

He leaned in, his heavy chest pressing against my back. His breath was hot on my neck.

His tongue snaked out, flicking across my skin. I moaned, squeezing my eyes shut.

"When you walked in yesterday, you didn't want this the same way I did. The same way that Dell did."

"I was scared," I answered, my breath hitching.

"Scared of monsters."

"Scared of love," I corrected. "Scared of feeling again.

How will I ever walk away from you now, Dracon? How will I ever walk away from Dell? I didn't believe in soul-mates until I met the two of you. I didn't believe the Barista could find me someone, and yet he found you and Dell. I didn't think I would ever be able to move on from the past, but I'm ready to. Even if it means changing," I said. My heart suddenly felt ten times lighter, the weight of fear lifting. "I'm a human, and you're a monster, and I can't think of a better combination. I'm yours."

His tongue paused, his body freezing for just a moment. He let out a soft, possessive growl and then lifted me. He rolled me over onto my back, onto the tabletop. His hands planted to either side of me, his mouth crushing mine. I wound my arms around him, leaning into the kiss.

I knew it in my heart. I could feel the rightness— the same feeling I'd felt with Cal, except much more intense.

We were only halfway through the weekend, and I'd already given myself to the dragons.

Dracon let out another soft growl and broke the kiss, looking down at me. His eyes glimmered, golden and warm. "I promise you that you'll always be safe with us," he said. "I promise you that another monster will never hurt you again. And I promise you that you will be loved and worshiped the way you deserve, Kat. I can't promise there won't be times I lose myself, and I can't promise that there won't be times I fuck up. But, god damn it, I know this is right. My dragon knows this is right. The whole world can think we're crazy. I don't even care. You belong with me. You belong with Dell."

I nodded, my eyes filling with tears.

"If I bond you, there's no going back," he whispered.

"I'll never go back. I want it, Dracon. Please."

How could I ever go back? Tomorrow was the last day

of our three day weekend, but I would never be able to go another day without knowing they were mine.

He stared at me for a beat and then succumbed, bowing his head. His lips caressed my neck, his tongue swirling around the base. His teeth began to sharpen, growing larger in his mouth. His pupils became black diamonds, the gold irises burning like torches. He hovered for a moment and then sunk his fangs into me.

The pain scalded me but was immediately soothed by the fiercest feeling of belonging I'd ever felt in my life. A scream died in my throat as I felt my soul slide into my dragon's hands.

He was a beast. He was a monster. He was a creature.

He was mine.

My blood was now streaming into his mouth, which was a strange feeling. He drank from me, a deep purr rattling his chest.

He drew back, and I watched the crimson drip down his chin. His forked tongue licked his lips slowly. "You taste..." he moaned, getting every last drop from his mouth, "...like a little sip of sin. Absolute perfection."

I reached up and pulled him towards me, eager for another kiss. I was greedy to taste him again, to feel his hot mouth on mine.

He scooped me up and stood, my legs wrapping around his waist.

"I'm going to breed you," he whispered.

The idea sent a lightning rod straight to my pussy. I let out a stunned breath.

I didn't know I had a breeding kink, but based on how my entire body was tingling now— I'd say I definitely had one.

I wound myself around him as he carried me through

the living room and down a staircase I hadn't noticed until now. It was shrouded in shadows, daylight leaving the space.

"Where's Dell?" I whispered as we plunged into darkness.

"He's scouting the area with two of the Barista's friends. You should be able to feel him now, through the bond."

My eyes widened at the thought.

Part of me wanted to panic at the idea of him being outside, but the presence of reassurance was stronger. Warmth spread through me as Dracon kicked open a door, his tail shoving it closed behind us.

"This room is a nest," he said softly.

I blinked, my vision adjusting. Dracon raised his head, and fire tumbled out of his mouth. I watched in awe as torches lit up around the room, just as Dell had done earlier.

"Shit," I whispered. "That's hot."

He snorted, smoke curling out of his nostrils. "That's nothing, little kitten."

He carried me to a massive pile of...blankets? At the center of the room were mounds of soft fabrics, all creating a wall around the center. It truly reminded me of a nest, one that was large enough for not one full-sized dragon but two.

Dracon laid me down at the center, and I looked between us, my eyes widening. I'd never get over the size of his cock. The uniqueness of it.

I licked my lips.

He chuckled. "Hold onto me, kitten. I want you to rake your nails across my back while I fuck you."

I wound my arms around his neck, my legs around his hips. The tip of his cock pressed against me, teasing me.

"You're so wet," he growled.

"Please fuck me," I whispered.

I felt his resistance finally cave. He pressed me against the soft blankets and shoved into me. I screamed as I arched against him, yelling as he filled me.

Every ridge that slipped inside of me brought a wave of pleasure. I moaned as he went to the hilt, stopping just at the knot. He waited for a moment, giving me time to adjust.

"Fuck me," I gasped, pinching his shoulder.

He snarled but finally listened. He began to pump in and out of me at a brutal pace, his muscles rippling.

Finally, he let out a soft groan and then gave a harsh shove, popping his knot inside of me. His seed immediately began to flow, filling me. I could feel the spurts of cream, a steady flow only interrupted by the sounds of his little grunts.

I let out another cry. This time, my nails did rake down his back.

His knot was huge. Even bigger than Dell's.

My entire body began to shake as an orgasm shattered me. Being tied to him, joined with him, filled with *him*... drove me absolutely insane.

"*Good girl*," he whispered, nuzzling my neck. "You're such a good girl, cumming around my knot. I can feel you dripping out. I can feel your entire body taking me, drinking my seed. Yielding to me."

His purrs made me cry out again, but this time he captured my mouth with his. He kissed me as he began to give more small thrusts.

"Fuck, there's no way I can cum again," I whined, clutching him.

How many times had it been since I'd set foot in this house? I'd lost track.

"That was only one," he laughed.

"One since we've been knotted," I hissed.

He snorted and stilled, his lips finding the place he'd bonded me at. He continued to nurse the bite, his tongue making me feel warm.

"Shit," I gasped.

"You're going to be tied to me for a while, darling, but I'm not going to stop fucking you. Your cunt is going to be raw," he rasped, his hand sliding to my throat. His talons wrapped around me, pushing me into the blankets. His eyes burned with pleasure, his lips parting.

His fangs glistened in the torchlight of the room.

"Look at you," he whispered. "A little dragon slut. All you want is *this*, huh?" His hips thrust, and I squealed, my body threatening to convulse again.

He grinned.

I narrowed my eyes at him. "You're heartless," I gasped.

He gave another thrust, and I moaned.

"Dracon!" I cried.

He was still cumming, his knot pulsing inside of me. All I could think of was him and how good everything felt.

He chuckled again and leaned forward, scooping me against him. He then rolled over onto his back, seating me on top.

"Rest," he whispered.

I relaxed, despite the fact that my blood was humming with damn good sex, and my pussy was still throbbing around him. I closed my eyes, pressing my face against his blue dragon scales.

He began to pet me, which put me to sleep rather quickly.

**DELL**

"There was someone definitely here."

I looked up at the massive gray werewolf named Al. The sky had turned from bright blue to bands of red and orange, the sun finally beginning to set.

"But you didn't see anyone?" Jasper asked.

Jasper was an Orc that rivaled even my height.

"I didn't, but I'd just been knotted. Sometimes our senses...." I trailed off, not really wanting to talk about *that* with these two random creatures. Friends of the Barista? Sure. Friends of mine? No.

Al snorted. "That makes more sense then. A whole army of pixies could be camping out here, and you wouldn't know if you'd just left a knot."

Jasper smirked, his tusks jutting out from his bottom lip. His skin was dark green, his hair pulled back into a dark braided tail.

Part of being a creature was never flinching when an 8

foot tall orc showed up on your doorstep wearing nothing but a loincloth and a sword.

Al fixed the glasses perched on his snout, looking around the clearing we were standing in. Al was a stark contrast to his more natural friend. He was a werewolf, completely shifted, but wearing nice slacks and a button-down fitted to his massive furry chest. The top button was loosened, allowing charcoal-colored fur to spill out. He crossed his arms. "Well, we have two options. You either leave, or you stay. We tracked his scent to here, its still fresh. He could still be around, but it's hard to find the trail again. The girl will be hunted until he's killed. And I wouldn't leave her alone. You said Dracon is with her, right?"

"Yes," I said, glancing back towards my house. I couldn't see it through the trees, but looking towards them still gave me comfort. It was no longer just an obelisk of loneliness.

It was a home for my mates.

"And they're eating pizza, right?"

I blinked.

No. They were *bonding*...

"Dell. He won't be able to protect her if he's fucking her," Jasper growled. "Can't you keep it in your pants?"

I raised an eyebrow, my gaze sliding down to his damn near exposed cock. "Really?"

He rolled his eyes. "Let's go back to the house. That pizza is probably still on the doorstep."

Fuck, it probably was.

My stomach clenched, my chest burning. The fire within me was growing stronger and stronger every moment we didn't find the wolf after Kat. The idea of someone hurting her could turn me into a monster.

The three of us took off for the house, moving through

the towering pines quickly. Cool shadows bathed my skin as I ran, the feathered branches clacking together in the wind.

My house stood bathed in peach lighting. A stack of pizzas sat on the front porch, making me groan just a little. I'd left my two mates unprotected and hadn't thought about it until Jasper had made his point.

Al stepped up onto the porch, his nose raised in the air. Between all of us, his ability to scent was the strongest.

His eyes narrowed. "Nothing recently," he said, grimacing. "Why don't the three of you stay somewhere else for a few days? Maybe moving will smoke him out."

I swallowed hard and lifted my face to the dying sun, letting out a sigh. "Our nest is here. With her being bonded to us...."

"Make a new nest," Jasper grumbled.

A growl swelled and then died in my throat.

That wasn't how that worked, but I wasn't going to try and explain that to an orc.

"How about you go check on the two of them, and then we all convene if they're able?" Al asked, cocking his head at me.

I nodded and moved to the door.

"Can I have a slice of pizza?" Jasper asked.

"Yes," I snorted, smiling to myself as I stepped inside.

The scent of sex hit me, making my mouth water. The living room was still a wreck, as was the kitchen. A small moan slipped out of my lips as I moved through the house, down the hallway to where I could feel their movements. Even through the walls, I could taste the buzz of euphoria.

My body was already beginning to shift more, responding to them. To their heat, to their need. To my own need.

Fuck. I wouldn't be able to keep them safe if I also fell into...

My thoughts drifted away as the door creaked open. My talons sharpened, my throat turning dry as I stepped into our nest.

Dracon and Kat were surrounded by mounds of blankets, their breaths filling the room. The torches on the walls burned with dragon fire, casting an amber glow on their gleaming bodies. Dracon was sprawled out with Kat on top of him, his arms around her.

A low growl came from him, and I licked my lips, my fangs sharpening.

"Come here," Dracon rasped.

I stopped for a moment, studying the two of them. They were still knotted, although Kat might have been asleep. I smirked as I stepped into the nest, lowering to all fours and crawling to Dracon.

"I can't join," I whispered.

Dracon didn't seem to hear me. He grabbed my face with his massive hands and yanked me into a kiss, crushing my mouth with his. I let out a soft moan, melting.

Kat lifted her head, her hooded gaze widening a little. "Dell," she groaned.

I drew back from Dracon, running my hand down her back. She shivered under my touch, heat blooming in her cheeks. "Hi kitten," I purred. "You look good."

"I am good," she mewled. Her hand slipped up my chest. "Come lay with us."

"I can't," I said, closing my eyes for a moment.

"Dell," Dracon growled.

"I can't," I said again, "I'm trying to keep the two of you from the wolf, god damn it."

Dracon growled again, his eyes narrowing. He started to shift, but Kat let out a little cry.

"How long have the two of you been like this?" I snorted, kissing the top of Kat's head.

"Three hours!" she exclaimed, looking up at me.

"It's not going down," Dracon said, referencing his still swollen knot.

"Hmmm." I slid down to study where they were joined, my own cock lurching at the sight. Kat was spread wide, her body like a glove around Dracon's massive knot.

I leaned in and ran my tongue over the base of it, tasting their cum. Dracon cried out, his body jerking from my touch. Kat moaned again.

I really wanted to join them.

I closed my eyes, trying to regain strength.

I could help them come apart if I could send Dracon over the edge again. He needed to be stimulated to cum more so that the swelling would go down.

I leaned in again and ran my tongue from his knot to Kat's entrance. Their gasps made me grin.

"Dell," Dracon growled.

I looked up at him, my eyes meeting his over the top of Kat's head.

His amber eyes burned into me, his lust turning all of my resolve to dust.

"God damn it," I hissed, but my hands were already falling to my waistband. I slid out of my clothes and threw them into part of the nest. My cock sprang free, already pulsing and ready for relief.

In one swift motion, Dracon rolled Kat beneath him. His wings unfurled, giving me the full glory of my mate. His muscles ripples as he splayed himself for me, still knotted to our woman. "Fuck me," Dracon bid, his fangs glinting. "Knot me while I knot her."

The dragon within rose up, a beast of passion and need consuming me. I let out a strangled noise and positioned myself behind the two of them. I lined up my cock with Dracon's ass, and he raised a brow as the tip brushed against him.

"I wish I could see," Kat whined.

Dracon laughed, his head tipping back. "You're a little pervert."

"I'm your pervert."

Dracon grinned, and I smiled too. I gripped his thighs and then, with one thrust, buried myself deep inside of him. His entire body responded, his grin dying and becoming the expression of someone consumed.

"*Harder*," he gasped, his burly arms wrapping around Kat as I began to take him.

My control snapped, and I began to pump in and out at a brutal pace, not even trying to my gentle. Kat's cries began to rise as Dracon started cumming again.

We'd end up with dragon pups at this rate.

The thought sent a primal thrill through me. I leaned in and sank my teeth into his shoulder, enjoying his deep moan. His blood filled my mouth, the three of our bonds tying our souls together. I could feel his and Kat's pleasure. She belonged to us and us alone.

I drew back, licking the crimson from my lips as finally- my knot pushed into Dracon, and I began to cum.

The three of us melted into a mess, our breaths coming out ragged as Dracon and I finally emptied our knots.

It took a while, but finally— Kat was able to slide out of Dracon's grip and roll to the side. I moaned but was able to free myself as well.

Kat let out a wheezed giggle. "That was...god, how could I ever go back to having sex with a human after that?"

I snorted, and Dracon peaked at her with one eye open, scowling.

Kat was beaming even though her muscles were visibly trembling.

"I'm hungry," Kat sighed, but she snuggled back against Dracon.

"I can bring you cold pizza," I offered, smirking. "And water. Give me just a few minutes, loves. Also, we have guests."

## Dragon

All three of us sat on the living room floor across from the wolf and orc that the Barista had sent. The orc had already devoured three pizzas out of the stack and was now drinking a bottle of wine like it was water.

He belched and lifted the bottle, his eyes narrowing. "This stuff is fruity and not in a good way."

Dell rolled his eyes. "Well, first of all, it's not meant to be consumed the way you are drinking it."

Kat snorted and leaned back against the sofa, her eyes fluttering. She had already almost fallen asleep twice, but Dell had given her a gentle shake before offering her more water and pizza.

This weekend had turned into...something. A dream? A nightmare?

I studied both of my mates and then the two strangers.

Both. I had never been happier in my life, but I had never been this worried either.

Dell was wearing a pair of gray sweatpants, and I smirked as Kat's eyes slid to his crotch. Her hair was swept back into a bun, one of my t-shirts swamping her.

It would almost feel normal except for the fact we were all concerned about a murderous werewolf.

"I'd like to scout the area," I said, looking straight at Al the werewolf.

He nodded slightly. "Indeed. If we don't find him...."

"Then the two of you should go," I said, pressing my lips together. "You and Jasper have been here for hours, and while I appreciate it, I'd hate to keep you from your own."

Jasper snorted. "We don't have our own, dragon. Save your concerns. But," he said, rolling to his feet and flashing me— which would be a mental image I'd never be able to burn from my mind.

"JASPER!" Al growled, wincing.

The orc shrugged and then smirked, his tusk-like fangs jutting out from his smile. "Prudes. Let's go hunt."

"Wait," Kat said, looking around at all of us. "This is—"

"There's no use arguing," I interrupted.

"Why don't we use me as bait?" she pressed.

"Absolutely not," I growled. "*Aboso-fucking-lutely* not."

Kat crossed her arms and glared at me. "First of all, you're not the boss of me."

"Kat," Dell murmured, giving her a pleading glance.

Al and Jasper looked at each other and then back at the three of us, then slowly went to the door. "We'll be outside," Al called.

The door opened and closed.

I shook my head. "No."

"Dracon, listen—"

"No."

"Why are you such an asshole?" she growled.

I leaned forward and cupped her face as gently as I could. Her fiery gaze softened just a bit.

"I can't risk your safety," I said.

"I don't want you to either," Dell said, swallowing hard.

"We want to get him to show himself so we can end him," Kat whispered, pulling away. It made my heartache. She got to her feet, looking down at the two of us. "It's the quickest and even safest way. I want this to be over so I can move on."

"Kat—"

"I'm a human, not an infant. I won't break as easily as you fear," she said, scowling. "We'll set a trap. It'll be him against four creatures and me."

I was silent. If she were anyone else, I would agree. We could use the wolf's crazed lust against him.

But she wasn't just anyone. And I didn't like the idea of Dell fighting the wolf either.

Dell snorted and reached for me, his hand gripping mine for just a moment. "Dracon, you can't control everyone. You're going to have to learn how to give in sometimes. I don't like this plan, but she's right. We can draw him out, end him, and move on with our lives. We could even enjoy tomorrow since it's almost upon us."

I closed my eyes for a moment, trying to clear up my thoughts.

I felt Kat come closer and opened them. She stepped up to me, taking my head and cradling me against her stomach. I froze and then gave in, pressing my face against her.

I breathed her in. I loved her beyond words. Tears filled my eyes for a moment, and I turned, looking at Dell. His green eyes widened for a moment, his breath hitching.

I loved both of them.

"Listen, dragons," Kat said, drawing out attention.

"Let's get rid of the wolf so we can go back to our nest in peace."

Finally, I gave in.

"Fine," I said softly, nuzzling her for a few moments longer. "Both of you are ridiculous."

Dell snorted and stole Kat from me, wrapping his arms around her hips and squeezing. "Sometimes bullying is necessary."

I chuckled and then stood, allowing my wings to unfurl behind me. "Alright, then. Let's get with those two and make a plan. I'm also ready for this to be over."

**KAT**

I'd learned a lot about myself in the last 48 hours. One of those things was that my body was capable of doing incredible things— aka, Dracon and Dell making me cum until my brain stopped working. Another thing I'd learned about myself is that sometime between the moment I stepped into Dell's house and now, my frozen heart had melted.

I still owed them both more about Cal. I still had so many things to learn about them— their pasts, what they wanted for their futures.

But, at the end of the day, the Barista had done it again.

And, surprisingly, I wasn't bitter about it.

I thought about everything as moonlight hit my back. Trees loomed in a circle around the clearing I was in, and the air was thick with the scent of pine. It was crisp outside now that the sun had fallen.

I was wrapped in a blanket from our nest, one that was

drowned in Dracon and Dell's scent. I buried my nose into it, aching for their arms to be back around me.

The waiting was killing me.

If this worked, then I would be free. Finally free.

Offering myself up as bait wasn't my favorite idea, but it was the one that offered the quickest solution. The future was mine, god damn it. I was meant to be with my two dragon shifters and live happily ever after.

My happily ever after had been stolen once before, but I would make damn sure it wouldn't happen again.

The sound of twigs cracking sent my heart racing. My shoulders stiffened, and I forced myself to continue to look ahead.

I felt him. The presence of a creature— the same one that had torn into the throat of my husband years ago. The same one that had destroyed me.

I squeezed my eyes shut as he crept closer. I could hear his breathing, followed by a low growl.

"You betrayed me."

Claws suddenly gripped my hair, yanking my head back. My eyes flew open, meeting the wolfish face of a murderous monster. His jaws snapped, his fangs bared.

"I killed him for you. So you could be mine. *Mine*. And you *mate* with two dragons," he snarled.

His grip tightened, and he hauled me, drawing out a scream from me. Tears filled my eyes, and I started to kick, my heart racing.

"Hold on," I squealed.

He froze, drawing my face close to his snout. His eyes burned into me, fueled with mad rage.

"Why do you want me?" I hissed. "I'm just a human."

"My human. I've watched you since you could walk. I've watched you grow and turn into a beautiful woman.

I've watched you your entire life. He wasn't worthy of you,"
he said, his growl surrounding me again.

"And you think you are?" I spat out, glaring at him.

"*No,*" a voice rumbled loudly. "*He's not.*"

I had known what the plan was, but no plan could actually prepare a girl for seeing a massive dragon come down
from the sky. I used the werewolf's surprise to twist out of
his grip and take off running.

A howl split the air, and I was tackled to the ground. I
rolled over with a scream, trying to shove the bastard off
of me.

Within a split second, the problem was taken care of
for me.

The werewolf was snapped up into the jaws of Dracon.
His brilliant blue form glittered in the moonlight, and even
though the sound of bones snapping surrounded me, I was
stunned by his massive beauty.

"Little darlin', we need to get you to the house," the
friendly orc said. His arms scooped me up, but I was still
watching my mate destroy the monster of my past.

Dell's dragon emerged from the woods, his rainbow
scales glinting too. My eyes widened as he grabbed ahold of
the werewolf's head and ripped.

"Oh shit," I gasped as blood sprayed like a loose water
hose. "I think I'm going to be sick."

"Princess, I'm getting you out of here so they can put
the bastard completely down. Come on," he grumbled.

I wasn't going to argue. Jasper took off running through
the forest, taking me far away from the red massacre. I
caught another glimpse, one that made me actually gag, and
then squeezed my eyes shut.

It had worked. He was dead. Gone.

I'd never known I was being stalked, and the idea made

me feel sick. The wolf had said he'd watched me for years. Since I could walk.

"You're crying, poor thing," Jasper huffed. "Oh, look who's here."

I lifted my head. Jasper had brought us back to the house, and standing on the front porch was none other than the Barista.

"Let me down," I whispered.

Jasper did as I said, and as soon as my feet hit the ground, I ran for the Barista. He picked me up into a bear hug, holding me close to him.

"Kat," he said gruffly, setting me down, "I'm sorry this happened."

"I thought he was gone," I said, looking up at him.

The Barista looked angry. He stared down at me, his hands falling to his side and curling into fists. His beard sparked for a moment, making me wonder if it was going to catch on fire.

"Someone seems to be interfering in my business, Kat. And trying to use people like you against me," he said, pressing his lips together. "I wanted to talk to you before your dragons get back."

I glanced back out into the forest, but I only saw Al and Jasper standing next to a car on the driveway. In the distance, I heard a roar echoing, and I felt the triumph reverberate through my bond with Dracon and Dell.

"They'll be back any moment. But I have something I need to ask you," the Barista said quickly. "Did anyone ever contact you about me? Or ask questions? Have you noticed anything off about anyone in your life?"

"No," I said, shaking my head. "No. And you know I keep to myself. You know I would never betray you, right?"

The Barista paused and then nodded. "I know. I trust

you. Will you let me know if anyone behaves in such a way?"

"Yes. But what do you think is happening?" I asked, frowning.

The Barista's eyes turned bright red, his irises gleaming as if there were fire trapped in them. The air went from chilly to heated, and I remembered that my friend was very much *not* human. "I think an old *friend* of mine is back." He then smiled, his ember gaze dying. "Your mates have returned."

I wanted to ask him more, but instead, I turned around. Dracon and Dell emerged from the trees in their half-shifted forms. I sucked in a breath, my heart going wild in my chest.

The two of them took off towards me, and I was scooped up against Dell's chest in a matter of seconds. Dracon's arms slipped around the both of us, his brows drawn tight.

"Kitten, you're never doing anything like that again," he growled.

I nodded. "Hopefully," I said, smiling softly.

"No. I mean never. I will lock you away in a tower far, far away."

I snorted and then grabbed his face, drawing him into a kiss. He stopped it, though, wincing.

"I would like to brush my teeth, kitten," he said. "Dell too..."

"Oh," I said, blinking. "Right. Oh god," I giggled.

Dracon pinched my nose and then looked up at the Barista, raising a brow. "Barista."

"Dracon," he said. "I do believe an entourage is headed this way. I may or may not have called Dante, which led to Rum overhearing things."

"Oh god—"

As if on cue, tires screeched in the driveway as a sleek car pulled up and stopped. My mouth dropped as three bodies piled out of the car, one of them hitting the ground and puking.

I looked up at Dell, but he was equally confused.

"Rum!" Dracon yelled, squeezing past us. "Don't barf on the driveway, you fucking bull!"

I giggled, and Dell's arms tightened. We watched as the minotaur on the ground got to his feet and then scooped Dracon up into an aggressive hug, swinging him around like he weighed nothing.

Dell snorted. "I didn't think he could be manhandled."

"Me neither," I grinned.

Goosebumps raised across my flesh as my eyes met the dark ones of a devil with crimson skin. He was absolutely gorgeous and breath—

"Kat," Dell growled. "Don't even look at him."

I rolled my eyes and patted his chest. "Put me down."

"No, you're mine," Dell said.

"You must be Kat!!"

Dell and I looked up to see a man headed towards us, a grin on his face. He was definitely the most human-looking, aside from his stomach, which made him look pregnant.

"PETER, DID I SAY YOU COULD WALK? Your feet have been killing you!" Dante roared, dashing towards the man named Peter.

It was like I was living in a circus. An alternate universe. One where men that were over 6 feet tall could be scooped up like they weighed nothing. Peter was promptly picked up by the devil, and I couldn't hear exactly what was said to him, but his cheeks turned scarlet.

Dracon and Rum joined our circle, although Rum still had Dracon in a headlock.

"Dante, Peter— these are my mates. Kat and Dell. Kat is a human like you, Peter, and equally as breakable," Dracon said.

"Hey!" I snapped, glaring at Dracon. The way his smile danced on his lips made me smirk, though.

Dell sighed and finally set me down, allowing me to stand on my own for once. His hand slid to my waist a bit protectively, but he held out his other hand to shake the crew. I glanced over my shoulder to where Jasper, Al, and the Barista were— all deep in conversation about something.

Rum let go of Dracon and then pulled Dell into a massive hug, followed by me.

"Welcome to our weird family! And don't listen to Dracon, Kat. His balls may have scales, but they still aren't made of steel," he bellowed, patting my head.

Peter was still held by Dante, but he offered me a smile. "Hi. Sorry, Dante is possessive."

"Protective," Dante corrected, rolling his eyes.

"*Possessive*," Dracon, Rum, and Peter said simultaneously.

Dante glowered for a moment but then caved and offered me a smile. "It's nice to meet both of you. Sorry that your weekend has been interrupted. I'm glad that the wolf is dead. Speaking of, Barista—"

We all turned around, and Rum scoffed. "What the fuck? Where did those three go?"

I wasn't nearly as surprised as the others, but then again — I knew how the Barista was. He would have magicked them away so he could do Barista things.

"I swear, that man is bizarre," Rum muttered.

"Agreed," Dell chuckled. "But he helped me, so I can't say I don't like him."

"Dante, can you put me down?" Peter sighed.

Dante shook his head. "No, not unless it's on a bed. You're almost due."

I fought the urge to raise both of my brows since no one was surprised, but Peter caught my flicker of curiosity.

"Perks of being mated to an incubus," he said, grinning, patting his stomach.

I smiled. I liked him already.

"Alright, so what happened?" Rum asked, grabbing Dracon's shoulder.

Dracon rolled his eyes. "None of you had to come, although I do appreciate it. There was just an issue with a crazy werewolf."

"An issue that led to the Barista lending you two of his men and you and Dell feasting on his body?" Dante asked, scowling.

"It was someone who stalked me since I was a child," I said, looking at the incubus. That shut him up pretty fast, although the announcement caused a ripple in my bond with Dell and Dracon.

"*What?*" Dell snapped.

"I didn't know. He told me when he attacked," I said, taking a steadying breath. It was hard to think about.

Dracon muttered a curse and then stepped towards me, drawing me into a hug. "He's gone forever, kitten," he murmured.

I nodded and buried my face in his chest, taking comfort.

My entire life had changed ever since I'd met Dracon and Dell. I could feel the weight of fear being lifted from my shoulders, the promise of a future together burning away all of the ice around my heart. I had never thought I would find someone to love, let alone two people, but I knew it was right.

The three of us were a team. Whatever life threw at us, we'd conquer it together.

"You're crying," Dracon whispered.

"Come on, love, let's go get some rest," Dell whispered.

I nodded and cast an apologetic look at the others. Rum shook his head, "We'll see you and Dell sometime next week, I'm sure. Come on, Dante, let's leave the three of them alone."

There were a few goodbyes exchanged, along with Rum hugging Dell and me again, before I finally made my way to the soft bed upstairs.

Dell and Dracon brushed their teeth and bathed before crawling in next to me. Dell shifted, the weight of his form causing the bed to shift as he curled up around Dracon and me.

I couldn't dream of anything as amazing as this. Being cuddled by two dragon men that would protect me forever — two men that loved me for me...

I breathed in the deepest breath I'd taken in my entire life and fell asleep in their arms.

**Three Months Later**

**Dell**

Dracon and I stared at the picture on my phone and then back at the small cage at the animal shelter.

Kat had sent us to sign all the adoption papers. She had picked out exactly which one she wanted, a cute little black cat.

She was finishing up her room while we were picking up our first addition to our little family. She and Dracon had moved in this week— each filling two empty bedrooms in my home. Gone were the silent ghosts, chased away by my mates.

I looked at the picture again and then shook my head.

*That* was not the cat on the other side of the cage.

"This is Biscuit," the lady who'd brought the cat up chimed. "She's a little old lady but very loving."

"Loving," Dracon echoed dryly.

I'd never seen an angrier creature in my entire life. Two bright green eyes glared at Dracon and me. I'd never seen a cat scowl before but its furless face folded in ways that shouldn't have been possible.

"Why is it furless?" Dracon asked, narrowing his eyes. "We were adopting a black kitten. Not a mole."

"Well, you see, ah...that kitten got adopted, but I swear Biscuit is basically a kitten at heart! She's sweet and loving and—"

Biscuit stared into my soul as the girl droned on about how amazing she was. I was now convinced Satan had a long lost pet, and this was it.

"We came to adopt a child, but I think we're going home with an angry babushka," I muttered, shaking my head.

Dracon snorted and then shrugged, pushing his finger into the cage. Biscuit battered his finger with paw swipes—making me wonder if cats were secretly trained to be MMA fighters or if that was just this naked one.

"Alright," Dracon said, smirking. "We've been tricked, but whatever. We'll take Biscuit. Save the kittens for the children," he sighed, lifting the cage off the table.

The girl seemed to let out a sigh of relief, which was alarming, but Dracon and I both let it go.

Really, we just wanted to get our adopted progeny and go home to our love.

We signed the last of the papers and then got into Dracon's car. Biscuit hissed at us a few times, making me chuckle.

"This is a terrible idea," I said as Dracon sped down the road.

He cracked an easy grin and shrugged. "Well, she's not

exactly what we signed up for, but...I really just want to see how Ghost reacts to her."

"Oh god," I snorted, twisting in my seat to stare at Biscuit.

She stared at me from the recesses of her cage, judging me like she was a goddess.

"I hope Kat isn't disappointed," I said, trailing off.

Biscuit glared at me and then blinked slowly, turning her gaze away.

"Well," Dracon snorted, "I doubt she will be. Plus, I'm sure the cat will warm up to us. Maybe even Inferna."

I grinned, thinking about Dante and Peter's newborn. We'd all gotten a taste of what it was like having a newborn — which was what led to the three of us deciding on caring for a cat first before having our own children.

Inferna was the cutest devil baby in the world. There wasn't a little girl more protected on earth than her. Between Dante, Rum, Dracon, the Barista, and I— whatever poor bastard fell for her when she grew up would be in for it.

"Speaking of Inferna," I said, "Tonight is our night to babysit, so hopefully, Biscuit doesn't hate babies."


Biscuit did not hate babies. In fact, Biscuit was only fond of two people in the universe now, and that was Kat and Inferna.

Kat slid up next to me, and we both stared down into the crib. Dracon was carefully measuring out bottles like a scientist, muttering to himself about Type A versus Type B blood benefits.

Biscuit was curled around Inferna and had already hissed at me when I tried to take her out.

"So, what happened at the shelter again? I thought we were getting a little—"

"We were tricked," I laughed. "But, it's fine."

"I mean— *I'm* fine with it," Kat giggled, laying her head on my shoulder.

"Alright, you three," Rum interrupted, bounding down the steps into the living room. Ghost followed behind him, but the massive hound refused to enter Biscuit's freshly claimed domain.

"Aw, Ghost," Kat whined, trying to beckon him.

Rum snorted. "He knows better. You got two devils in that crib, not one."

Dracon snorted. "How did we get talked into this again?" he asked.

Rum grinned, "Well, I'm going to pay the Barista a visit, and Dante and Peter need some time together. I think Dante has developed a strand of gray hair, and Peter is soothing him," he said with a wink.

"Why are you visiting the Barista?" Kat teased, wiggling a brow.

Rum acted like he didn't hear her and waved at us, bounding out the door.

Ghost sighed and then laid his massive body on the floor, watching us.

"Well, then," Kat laughed. "Rum is something."

"He is," I agreed, smiling. I slid my arms around Kat and pulled her close. "Maybe he'll find someone now."

"If the Barista is willing to help," she said, her brows drawing together.

I glanced at Dracon. He had paused, his eyes flickering with the same worry I felt. Whoever was after the Barista wouldn't stop.

But, for the time being, all of us were safe.

Love between monsters and humans was dangerous, especially in a world that frowned upon such things. While it was true that creatures deserved love, too, it was also true that not all creatures were capable of such a thing.

Some were too far gone, like the wolf that had gone after Kat.

"I love you," Kat whispered. "I'm so happy with both of you. And honestly, I hope that the Barista will help Rum. Even if it brings trouble to us again. Everyone deserves to feel *this*."

Dracon set the bottles down and stood, moving to the two of us and drawing us into a hug.

The three of us stood entangled, watching Inferna and Biscuit like happy parents.

I was a dragon, a monster, a creature. I was many things — some bad and some good. But at the end of the day, I would forever be Kat and Dracon's mate.

**Hello**, my little monster loving **creature**.
I'm happy to say that Kat, Dracon, and Dell lived happily ever after with Biscuit and their new mismatched family.
But my job isn't over yet.
A minotaur has come to me. He's seen what love can do and he wants to have it for himself.
He wants to find the missing half of his soul.
And he's asked me to do it for him.
He's asked me to find him a **Little Lick of Lust.**
Come over to Creature Cafe to read about what happens next.

**Sincerely,**
**The Barista**

## Hello Creatures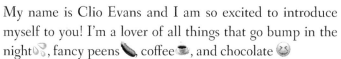

My name is Clio Evans and I am so excited to introduce myself to you! I'm a lover of all things that go bump in the night🐺, fancy peens🍆, coffee☕, and chocolate 😆

IF you had the chance to be matched with a monster- what kind would you choose?!

Let me know by joining me on FB and Instagram. I'm a sucker for werewolves to this day

P.S.

Join my Newsletter by clicking here- I won't spam you, but I will offer you fun rewards for being one of my monster loving creatures.

Clio's Creature Newsletter